Daddy, could I please have an ice cream, pleeeease?!
OK, I don't see why not.
OPEN

One swirl soft-serve on a cone, please.
Yes, sir!
CLOSED

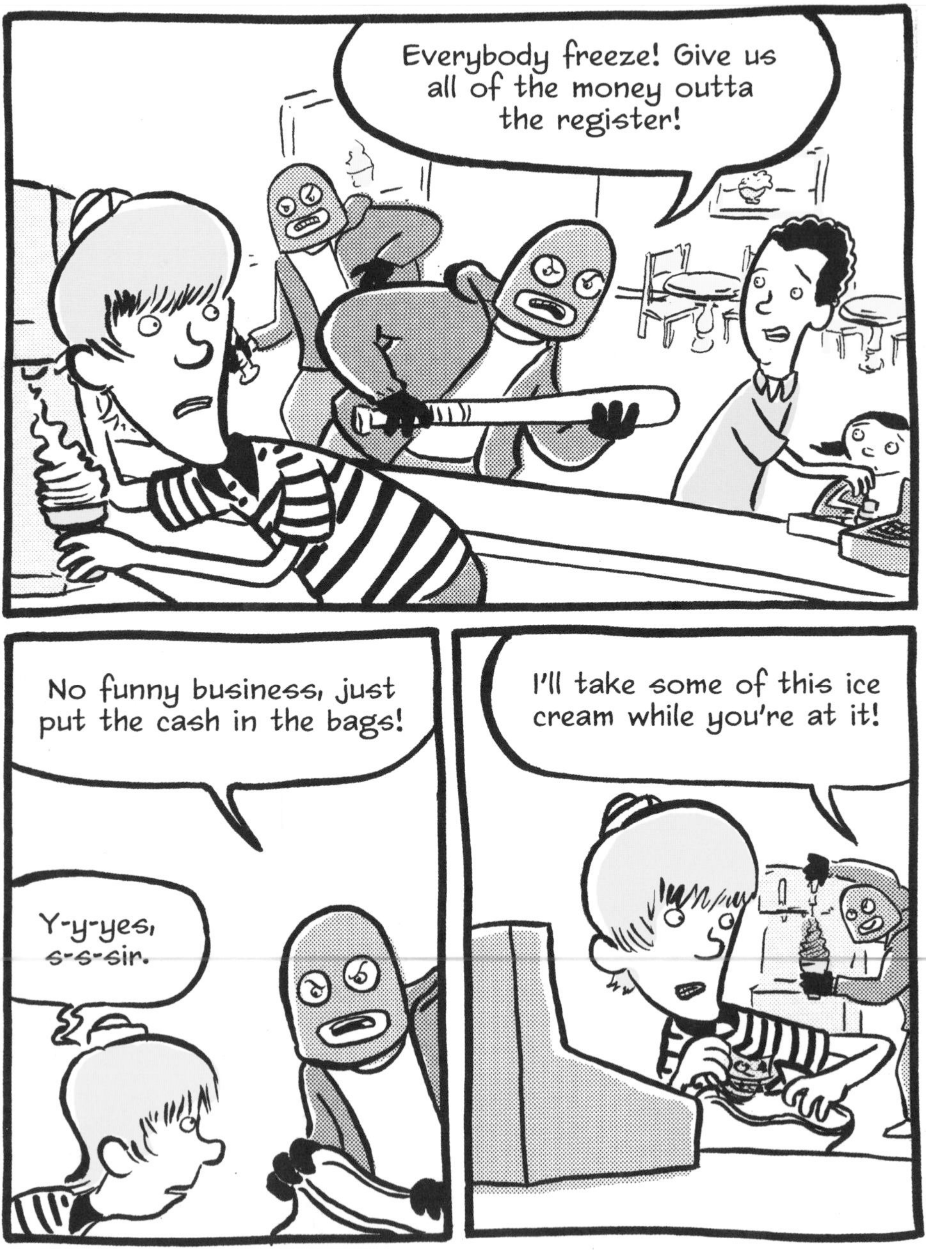
Everybody freeze! Give us all of the money outta the register!
No funny business, just put the cash in the bags!
Y-y-yes, s-s-sir.
I'll take some of this ice cream while you're at it!

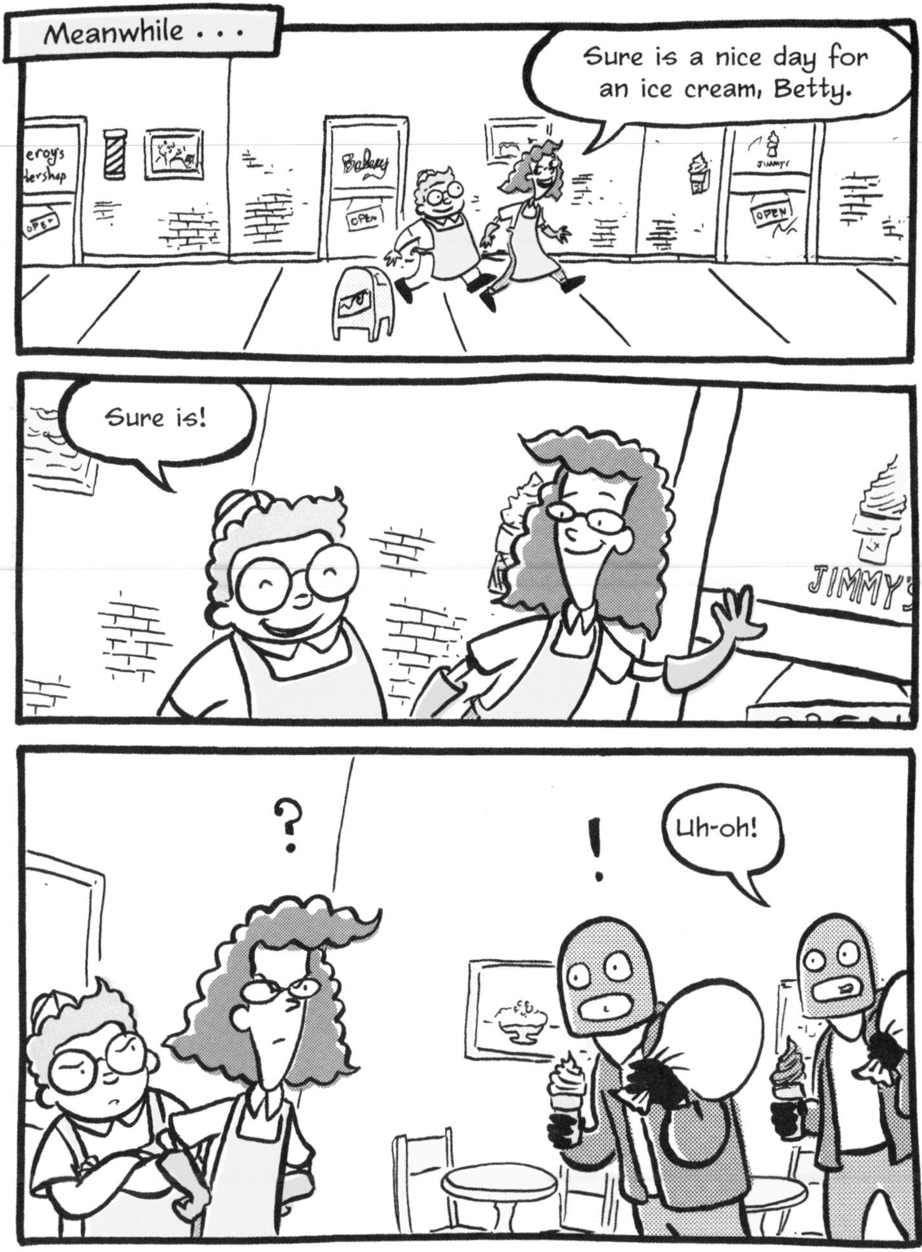

Meanwhile . . .
Sure is a nice day for an ice cream, Betty.
OPEN
Sure is!
JIMMY'S
?
!
Uh-oh!

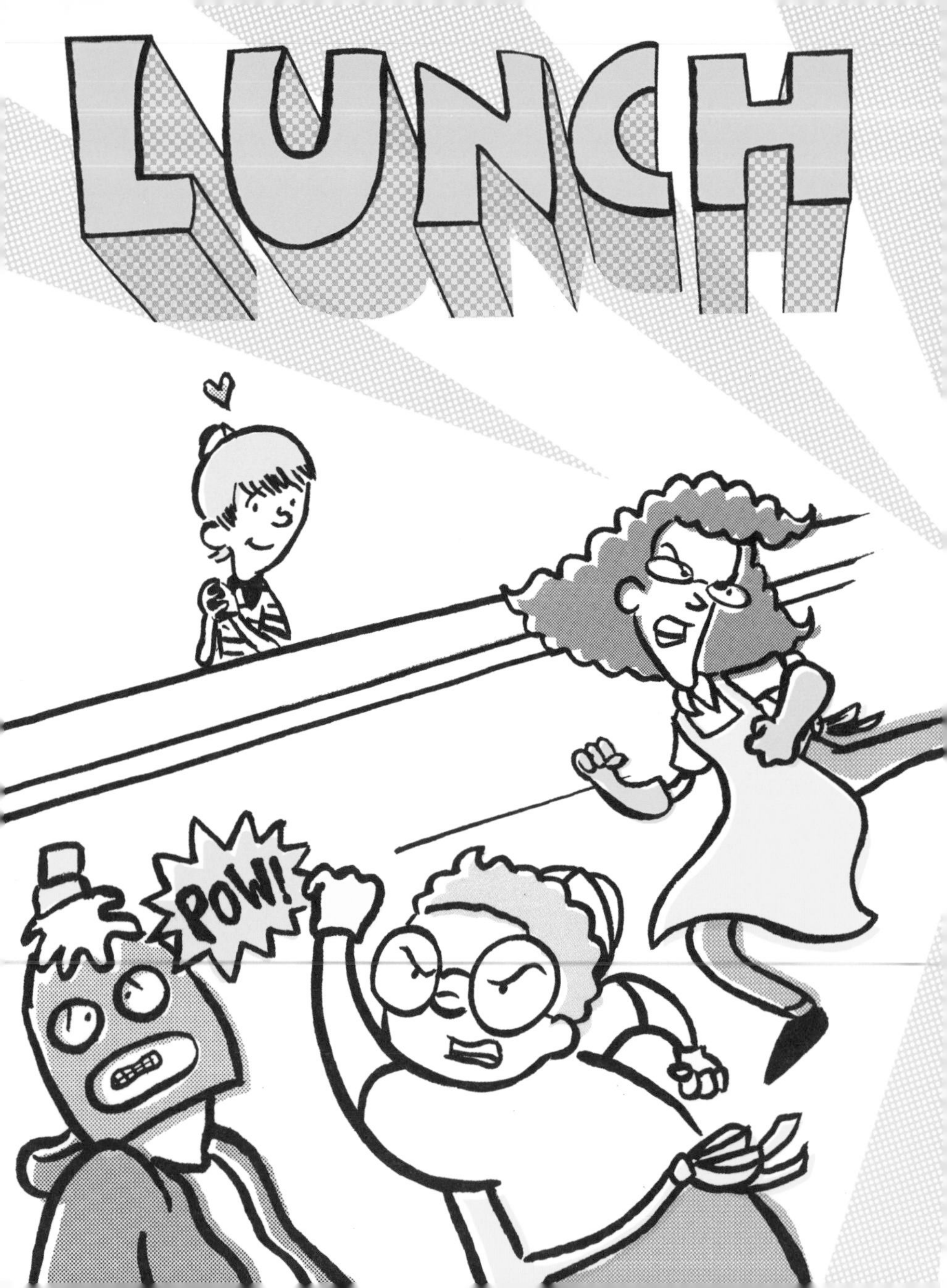
LUNCH
POW!

# LADY and the Mutant Mathletes

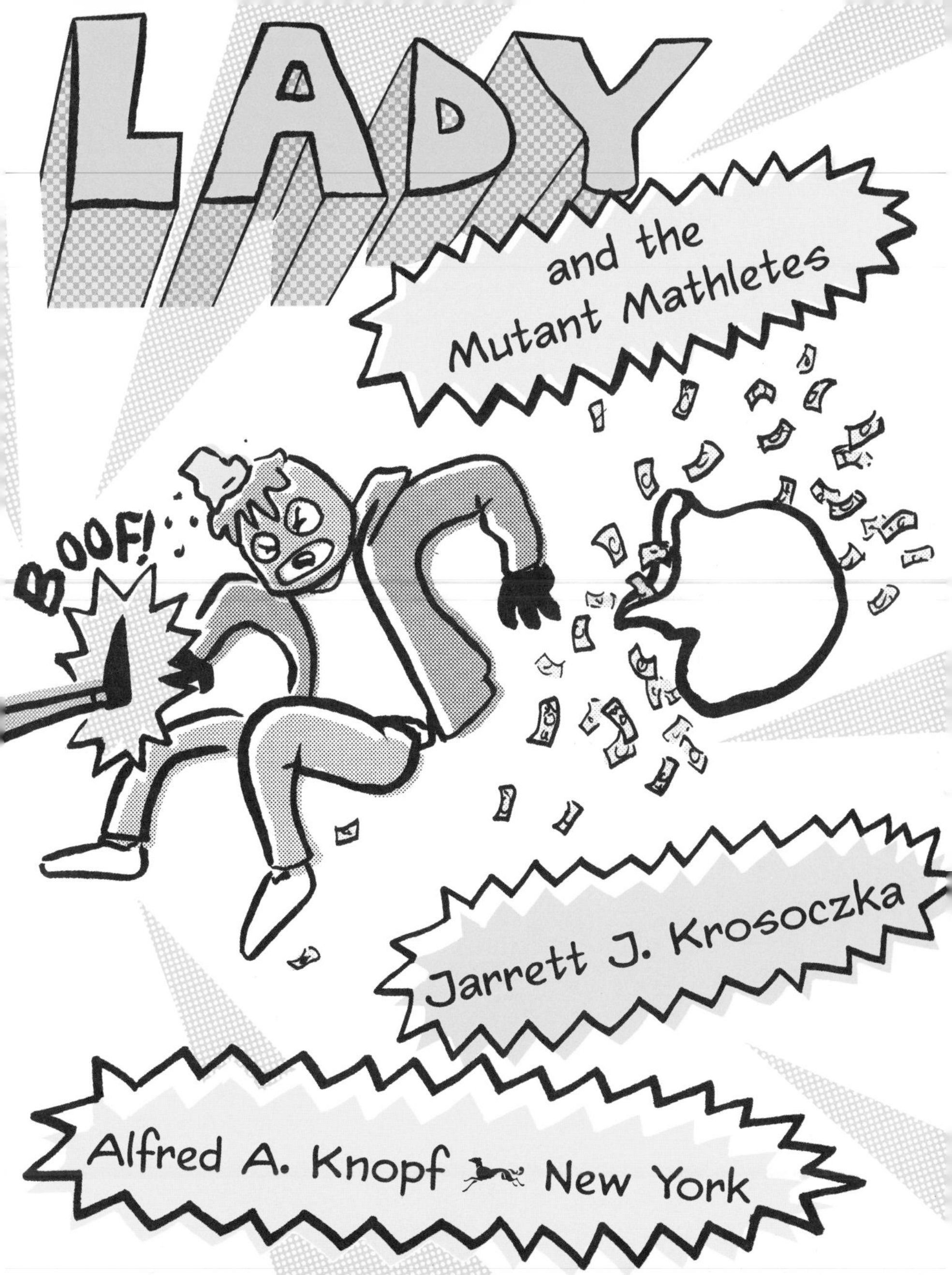
BOOF!

Jarrett J. Krosoczka

Alfred A. Knopf New York

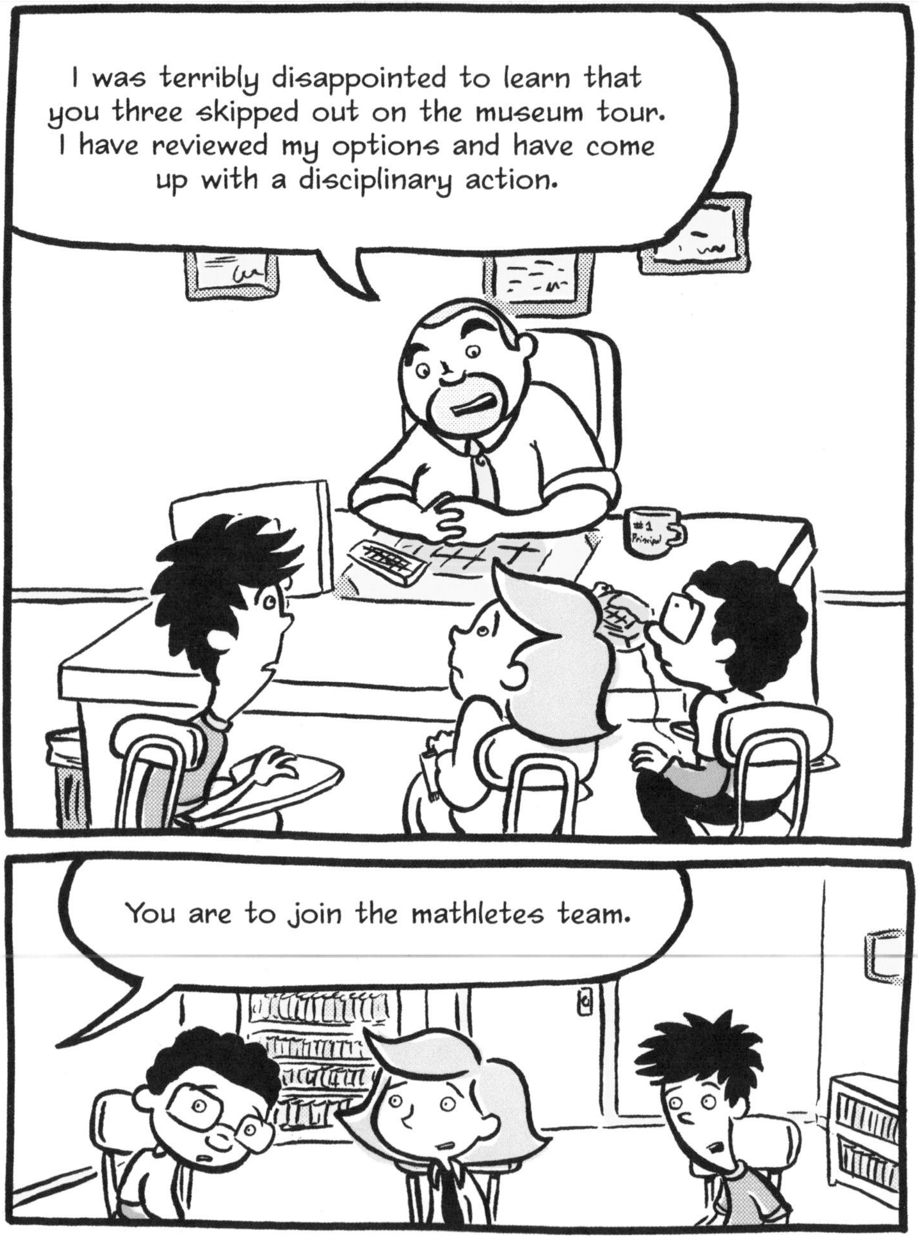
I was terribly disappointed to learn that you three skipped out on the museum tour. I have reviewed my options and have come up with a disciplinary action.
#1 Principal
You are to join the mathletes team.

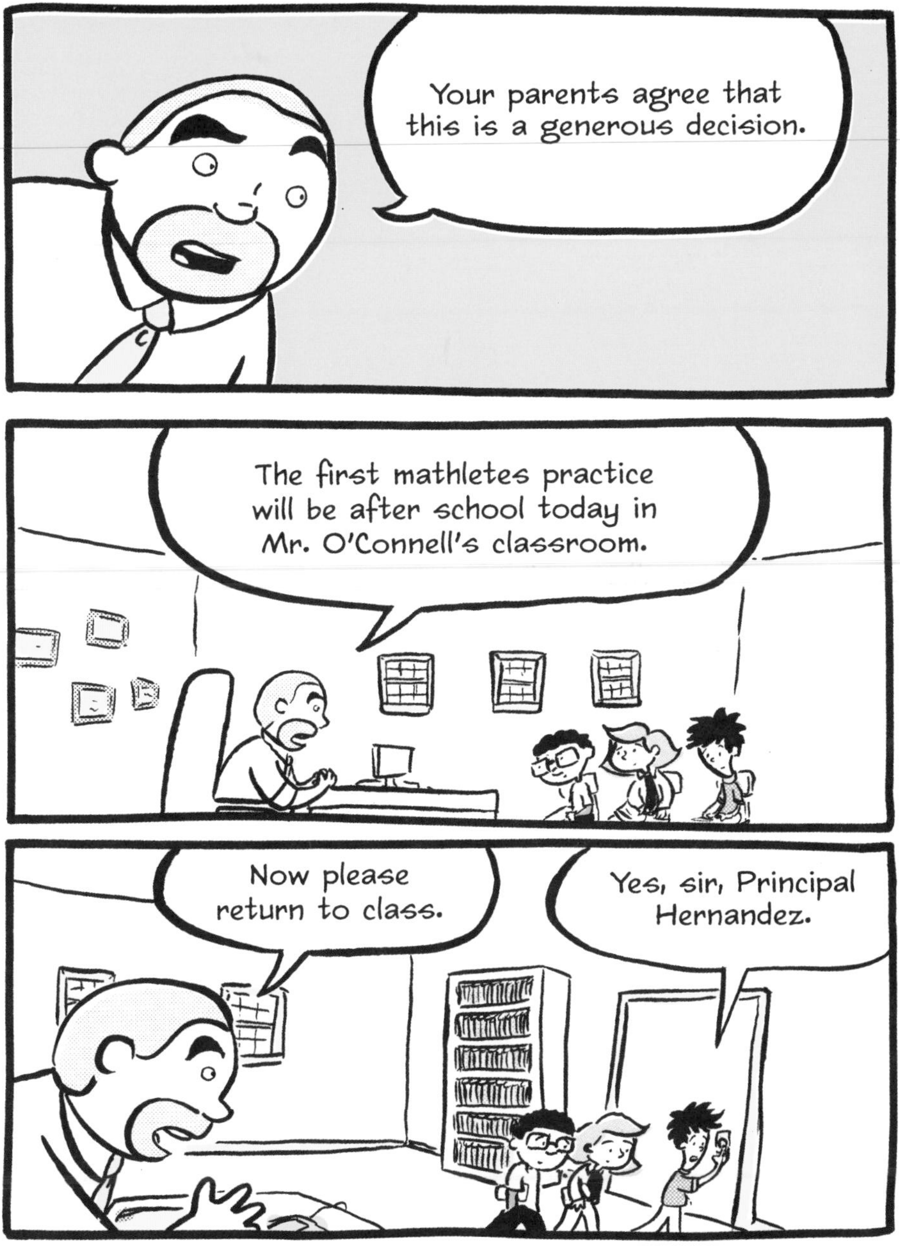
Your parents agree that this is a generous decision.
The first mathletes practice will be after school today in Mr. O'Connell's classroom.
Now please return to class.
Yes, sir, Principal Hernandez.

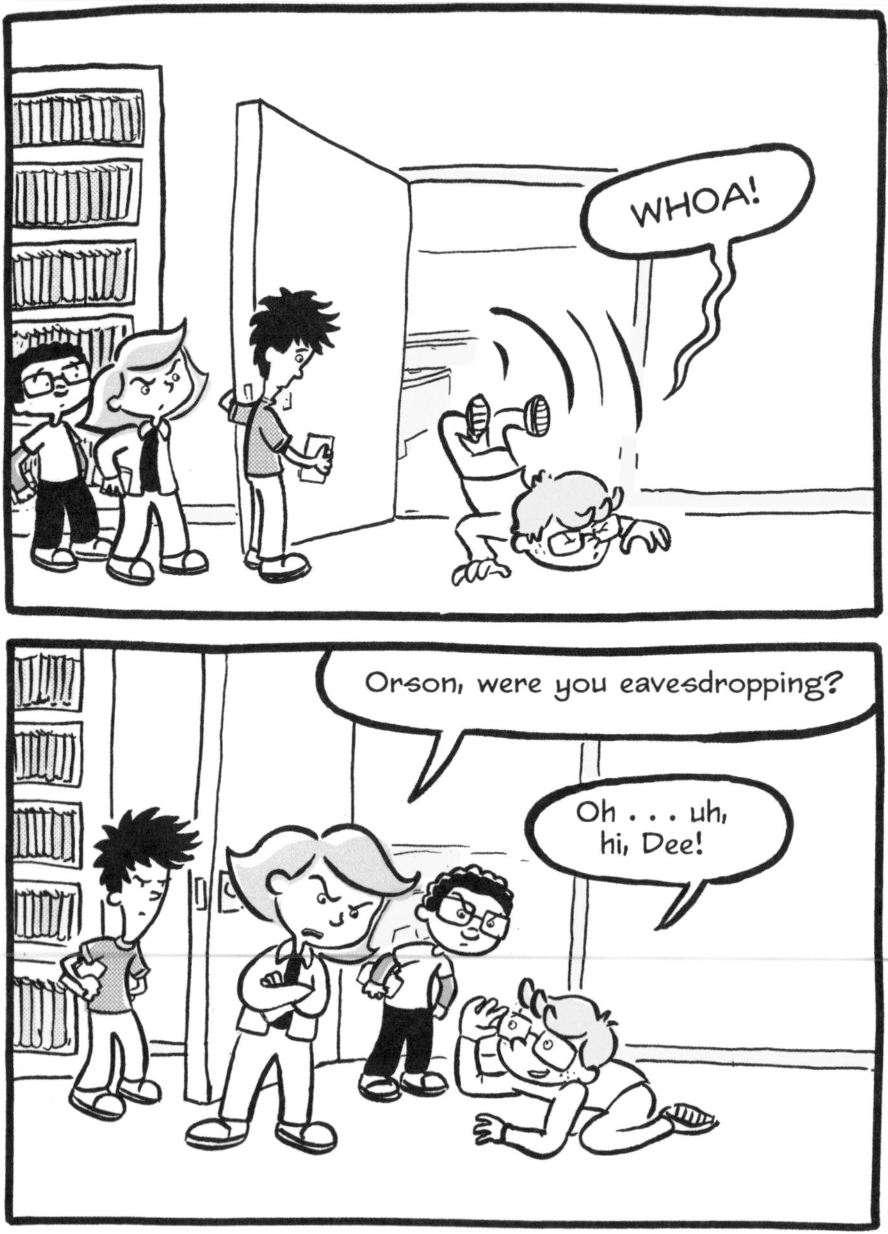
WHOA!
Orson, were you eavesdropping?
Oh . . . uh, hi, Dee!

Eavesdropping? No! I volunteer to help sharpen Secretary Louanne's pencils.
Thanks, sweetie!

See you guys at Mathletes!
TEAMWORK
PERSEVERANCE

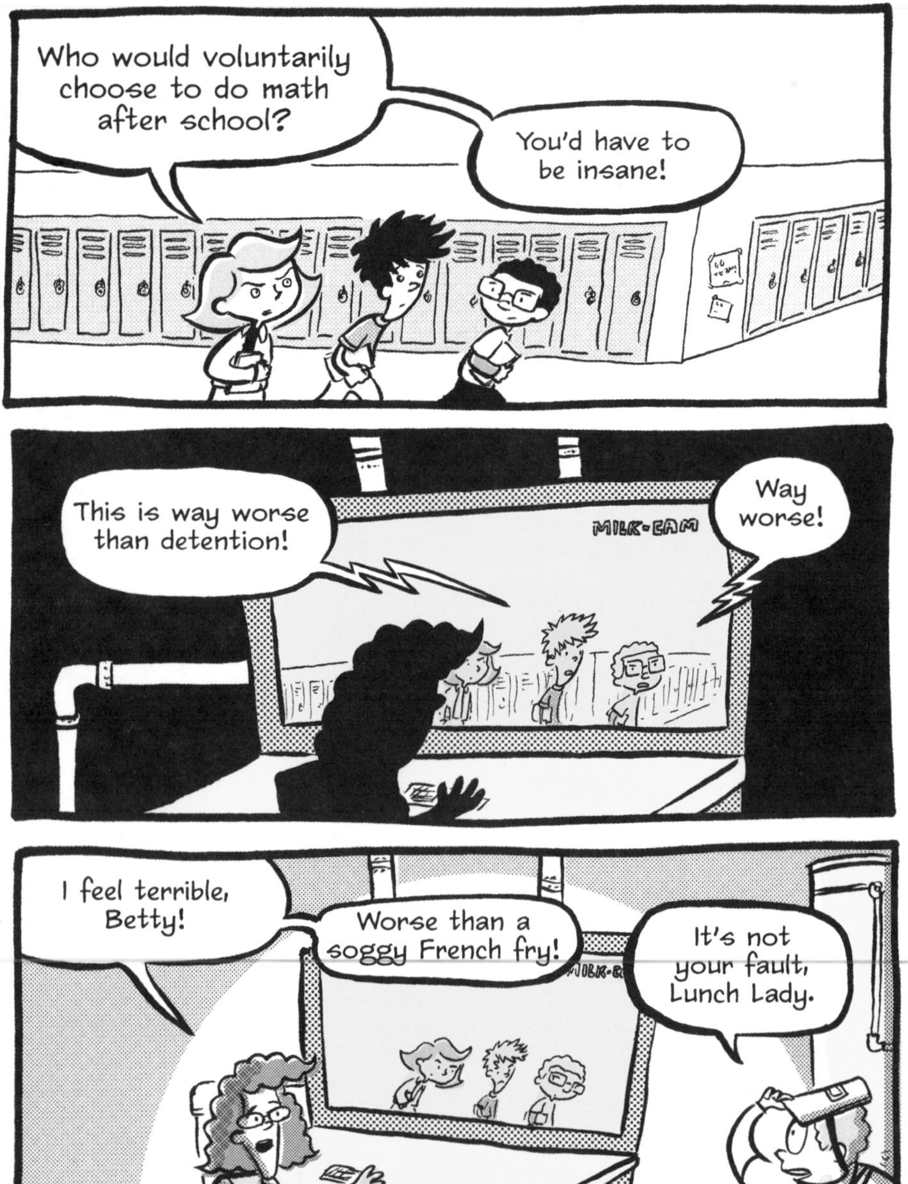
Who would voluntarily choose to do math after school?
You'd have to be insane!
GO TEAM!
This is way worse than detention!
MILK-CAM
Way worse!
I feel terrible, Betty!
Worse than a soggy French fry!
It's not your fault, Lunch Lady.

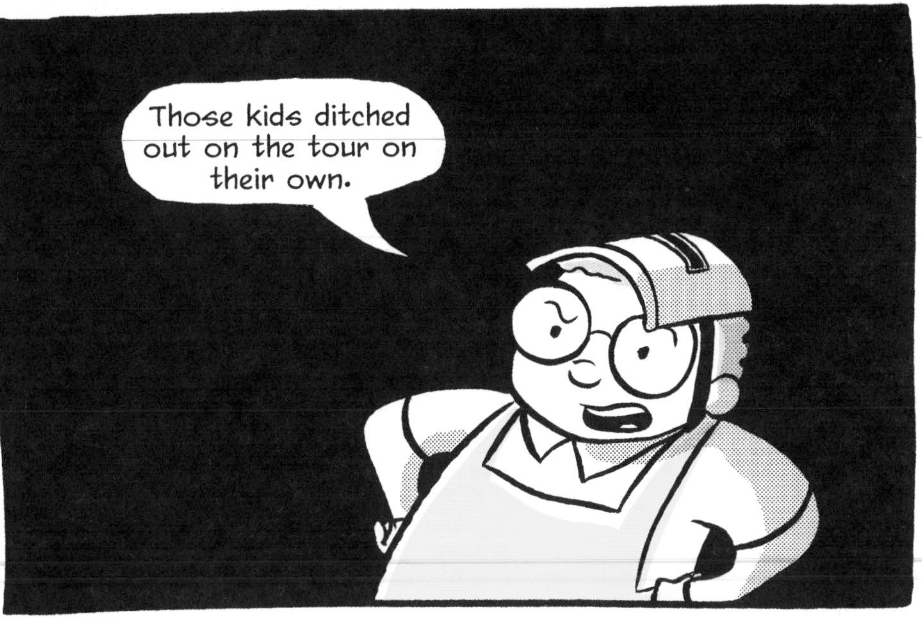
Those kids ditched out on the tour on their own.

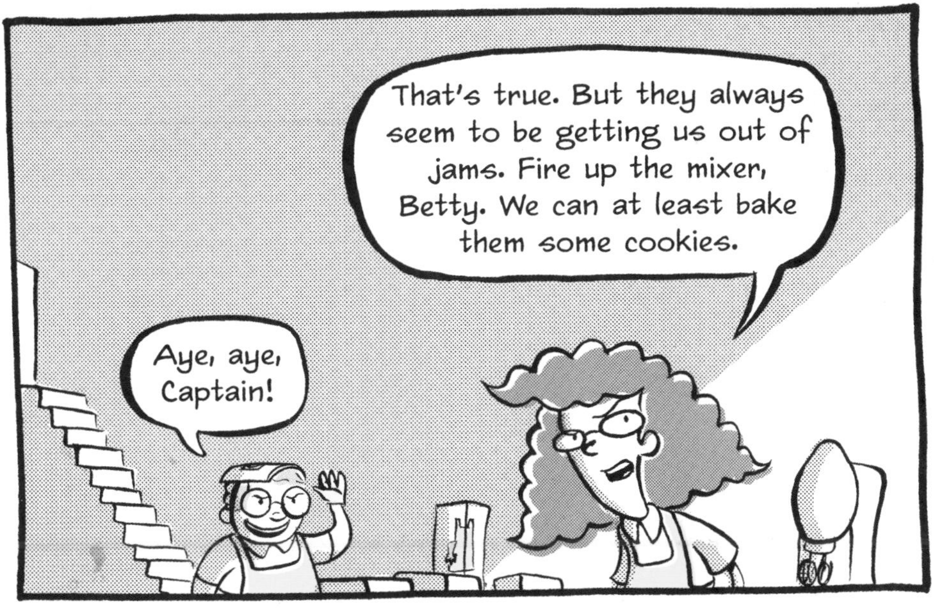
That's true. But they always seem to be getting us out of jams. Fire up the mixer, Betty. We can at least bake them some cookies.
Aye, aye, Captain!

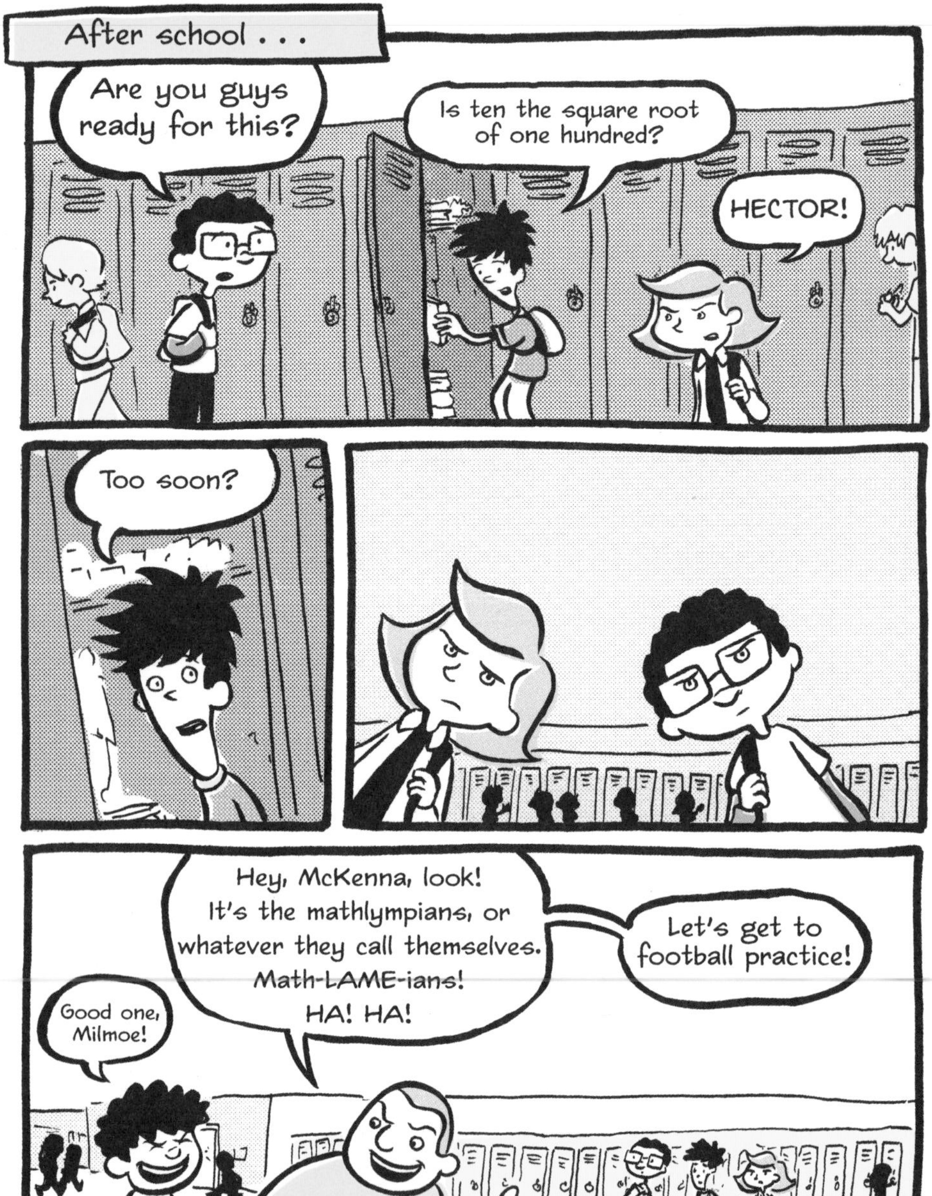
After school . . .
Are you guys ready for this?
Is ten the square root of one hundred?
HECTOR!
Too soon?
Hey, McKenna, look! It's the mathlympians, or whatever they call themselves. Math-LAME-ians! HA! HA!
Let's get to football practice!
Good one, Milmoe!
15

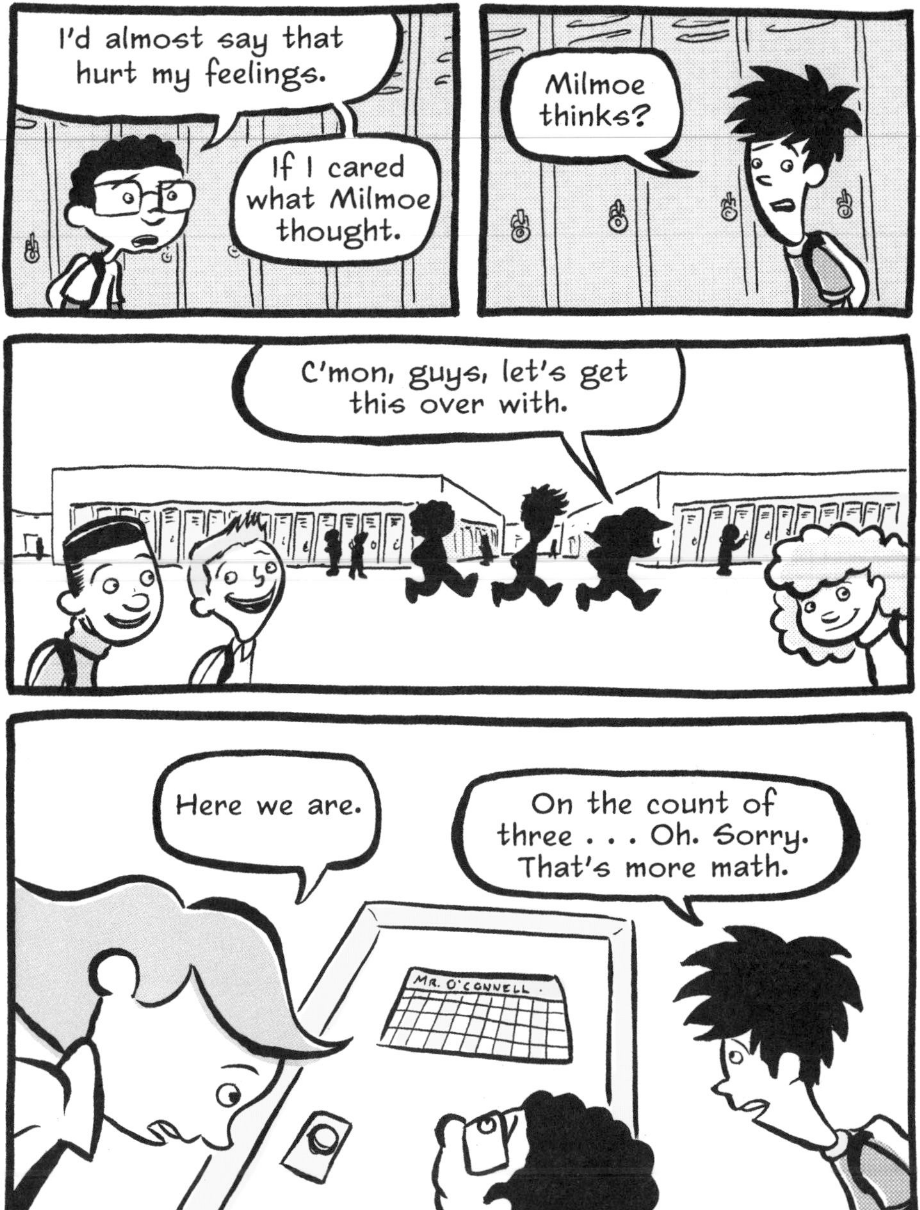
I'd almost say that hurt my feelings.
If I cared what Milmoe thought.
Milmoe thinks?
C'mon, guys, let's get this over with.
Here we are.
MR. O'CONNELL
On the count of three . . . Oh. Sorry. That's more math.

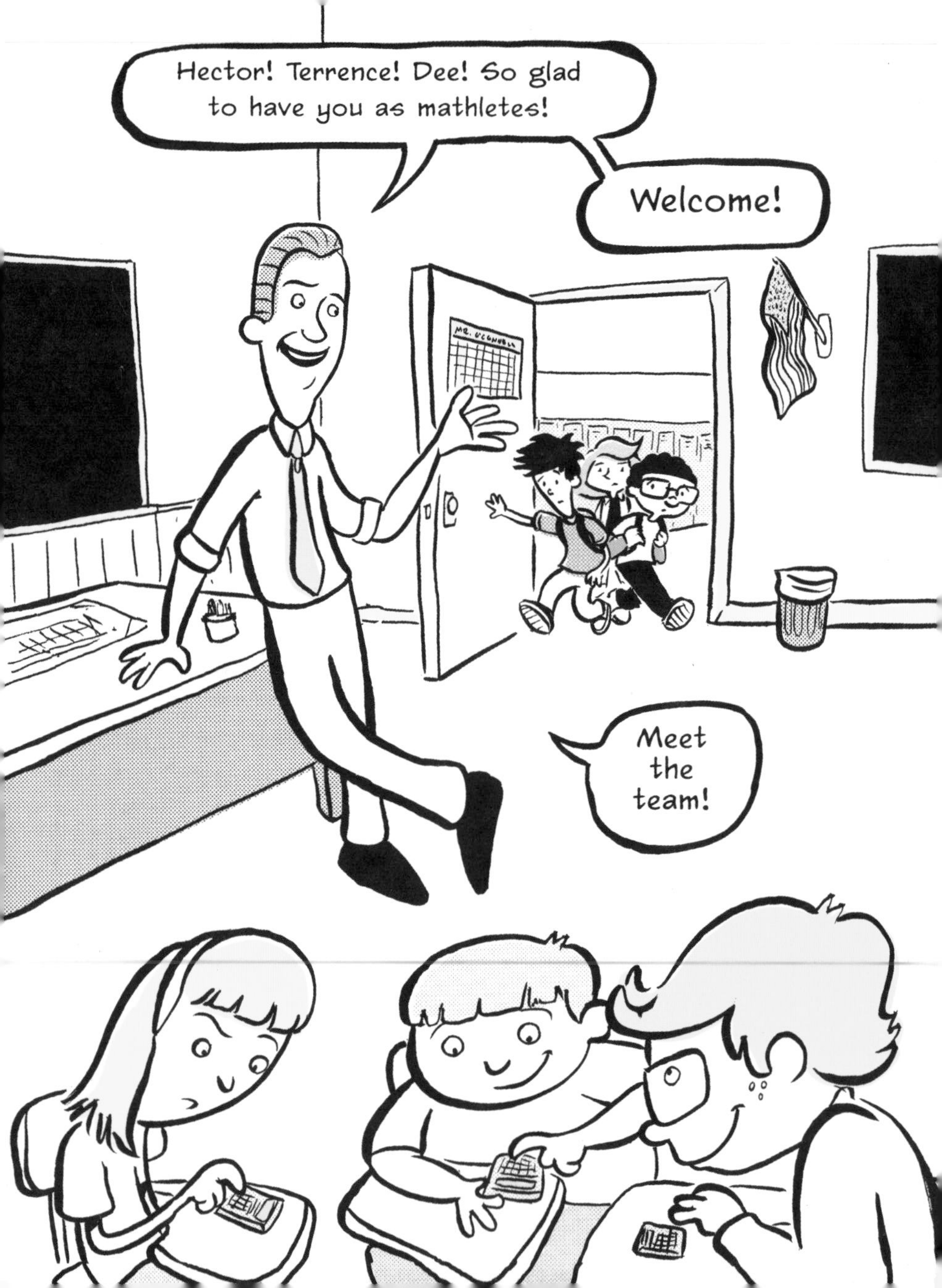
Hector! Terrence! Dee! So glad to have you as mathletes!
Welcome!
Meet the team!

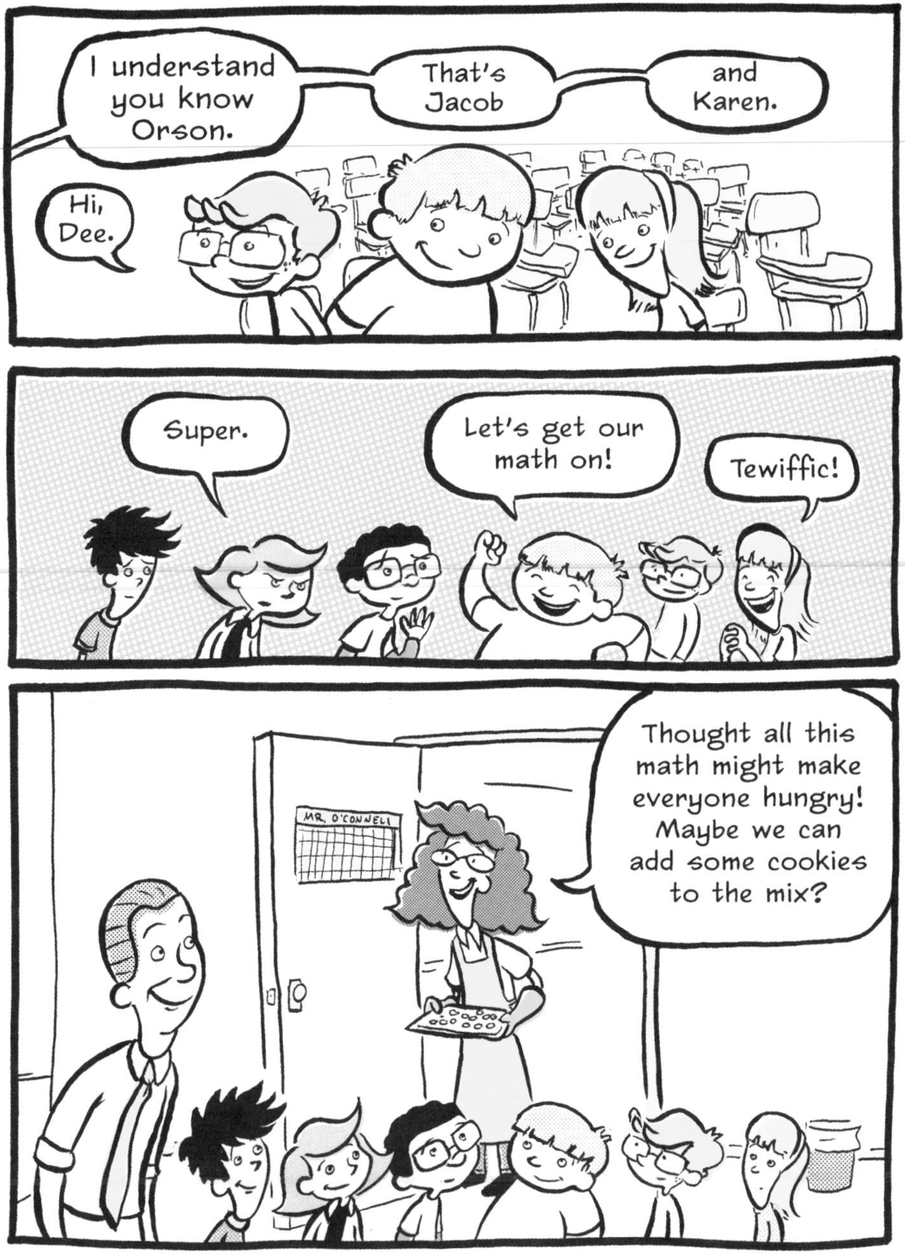
I understand you know Orson.
That's Jacob
and Karen.
Hi, Dee.
Super.
Let's get our math on!
Tewiffic!
MR. O'CONNELL
Thought all this math might make everyone hungry! Maybe we can add some cookies to the mix?

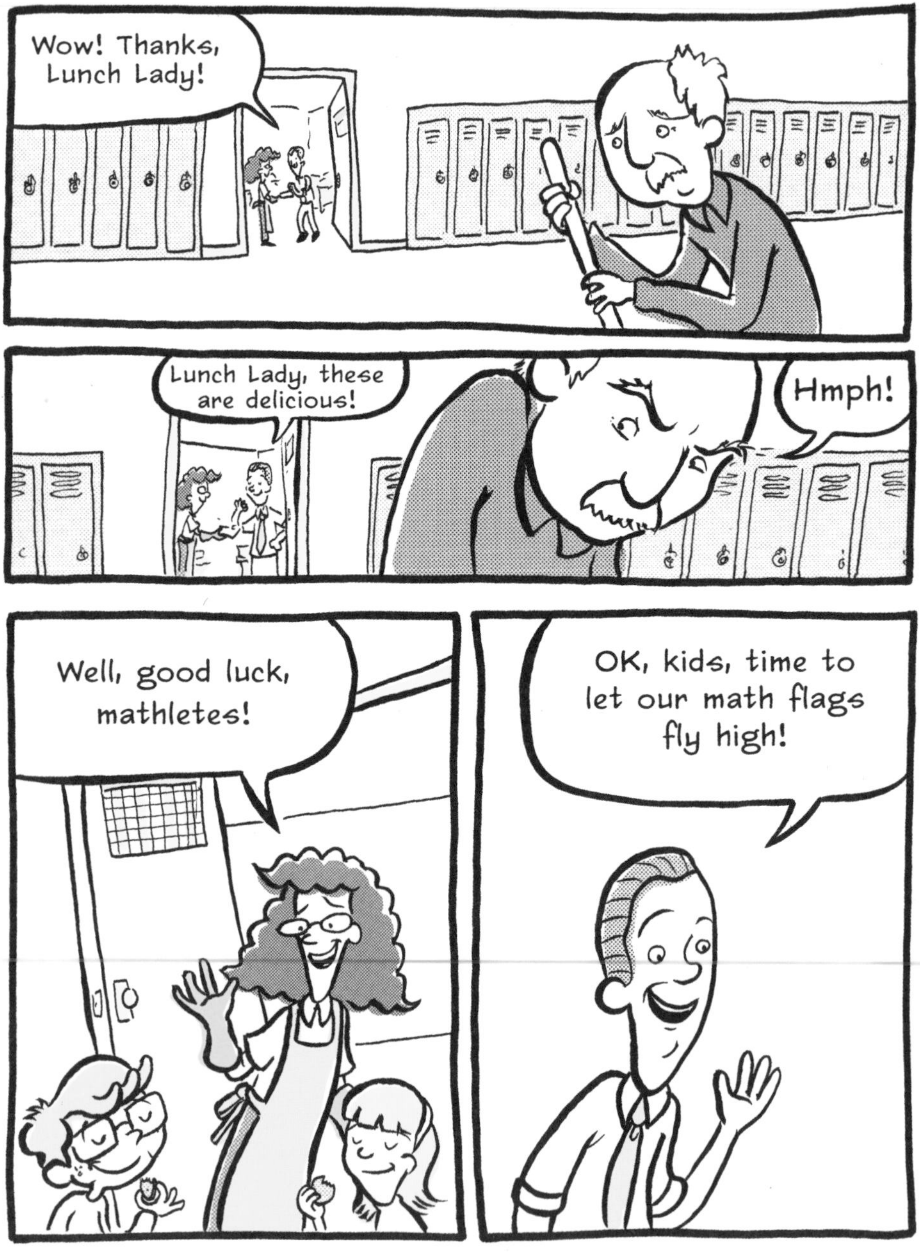
Wow! Thanks, Lunch Lady!
Lunch Lady, these are delicious!
Hmph!
Well, good luck, mathletes!
OK, kids, time to let our math flags fly high!

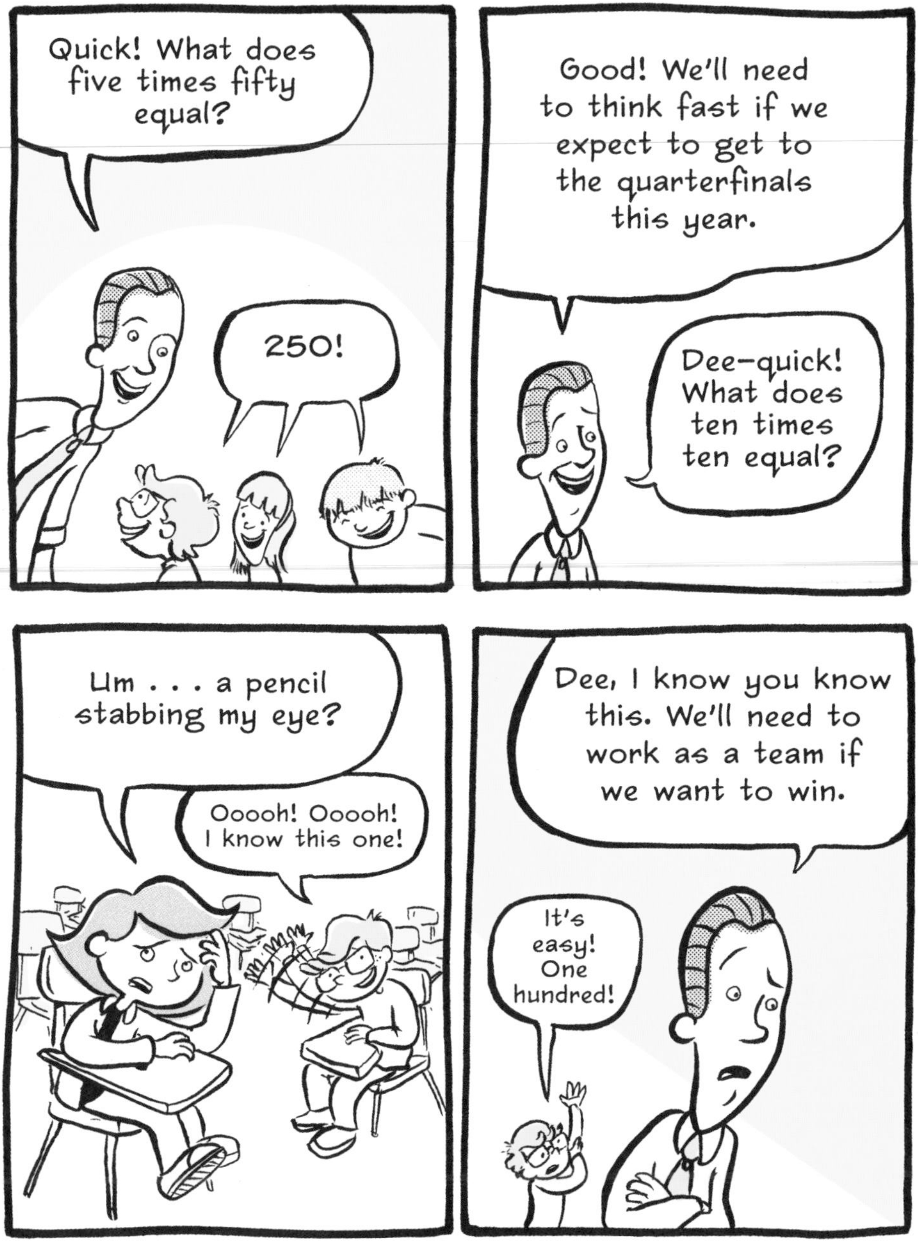
Quick! What does five times fifty equal?
250!
Good! We'll need to think fast if we expect to get to the quarterfinals this year.
Dee-quick! What does ten times ten equal?
Um . . . a pencil stabbing my eye?
Ooooh! Ooooh! I know this one!
Dee, I know you know this. We'll need to work as a team if we want to win.
It's easy! One hundred!

The next day at breakfast . . .
Good morning, Breakfast Bunch! How did it go yesterday?
The cookies were good.
It was painful!
The punishment does not fit the crime!

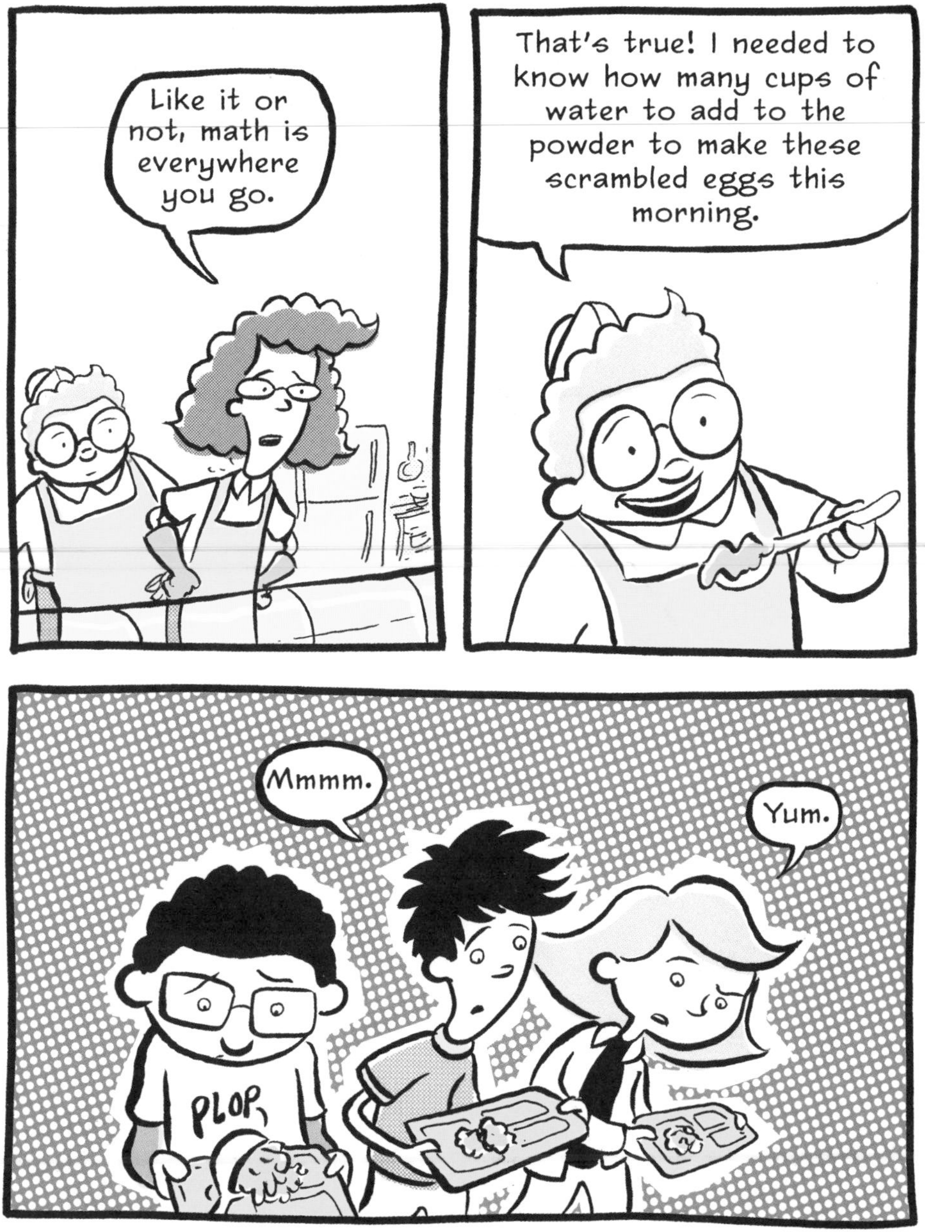
Like it or not, math is everywhere you go.
That's true! I needed to know how many cups of water to add to the powder to make these scrambled eggs this morning.
Mmmm.
Yum.
PLOP,

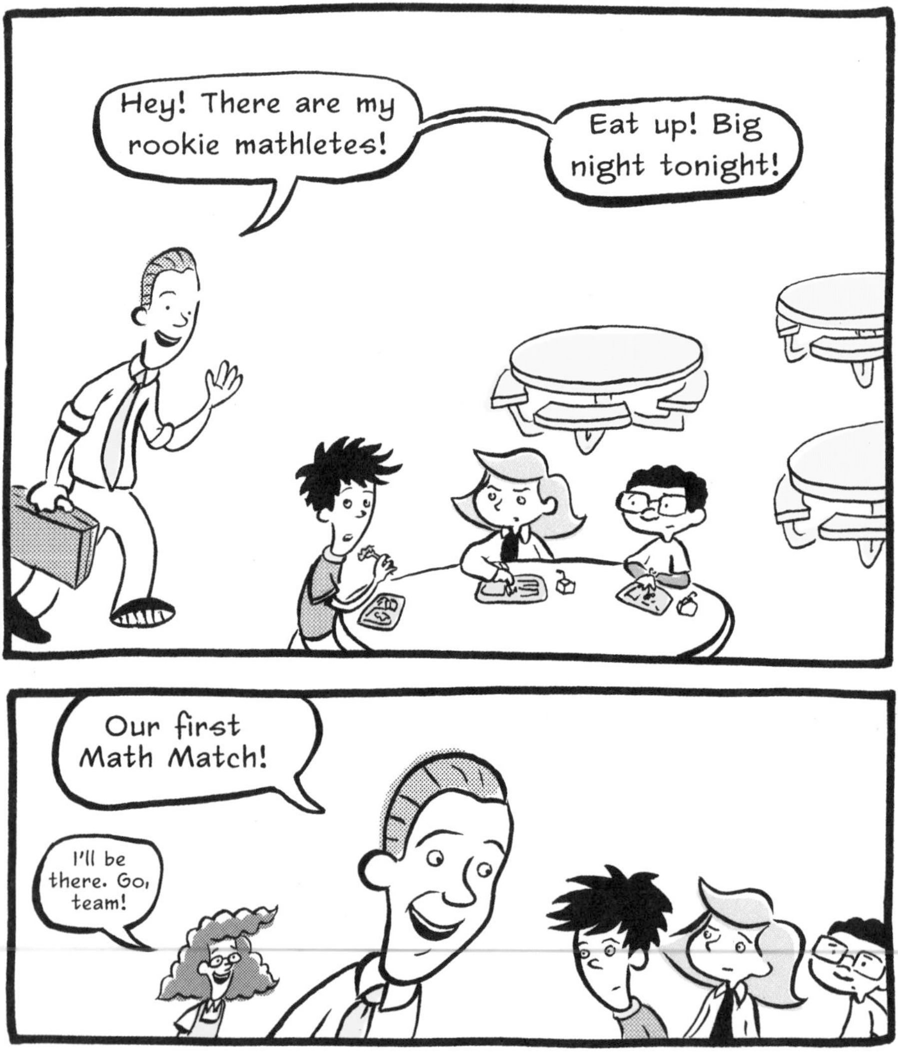
Hey! There are my rookie mathletes!
Eat up! Big night tonight!
Our first Math Match!
I'll be there. Go, team!
BRRRIIIIIIINNG

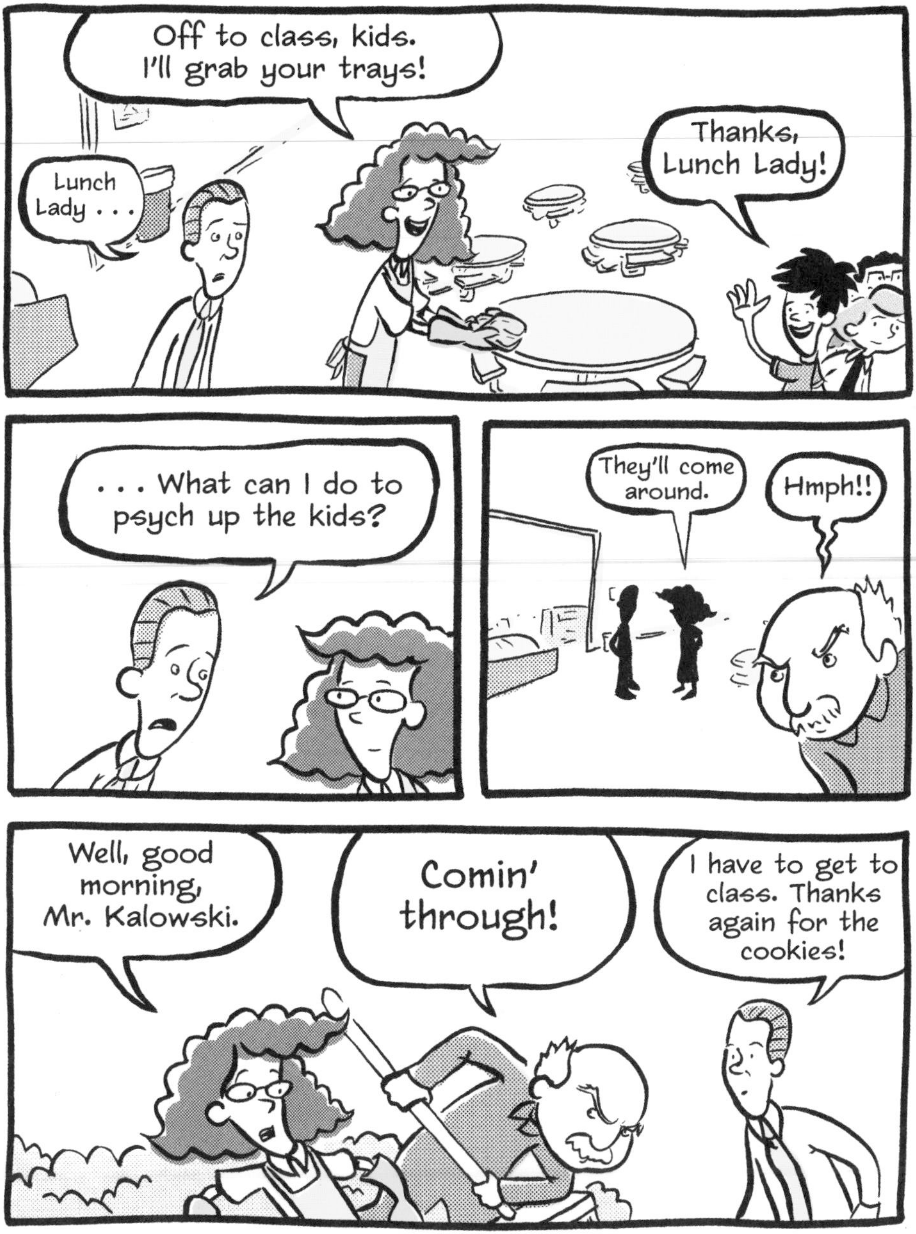
Off to class, kids. I'll grab your trays!
Lunch Lady . . .
Thanks, Lunch Lady!
. . . What can I do to psych up the kids?
They'll come around.
Hmph!!
Well, good morning, Mr. Kalowski.
Comin' through!
I have to get to class. Thanks again for the cookies!

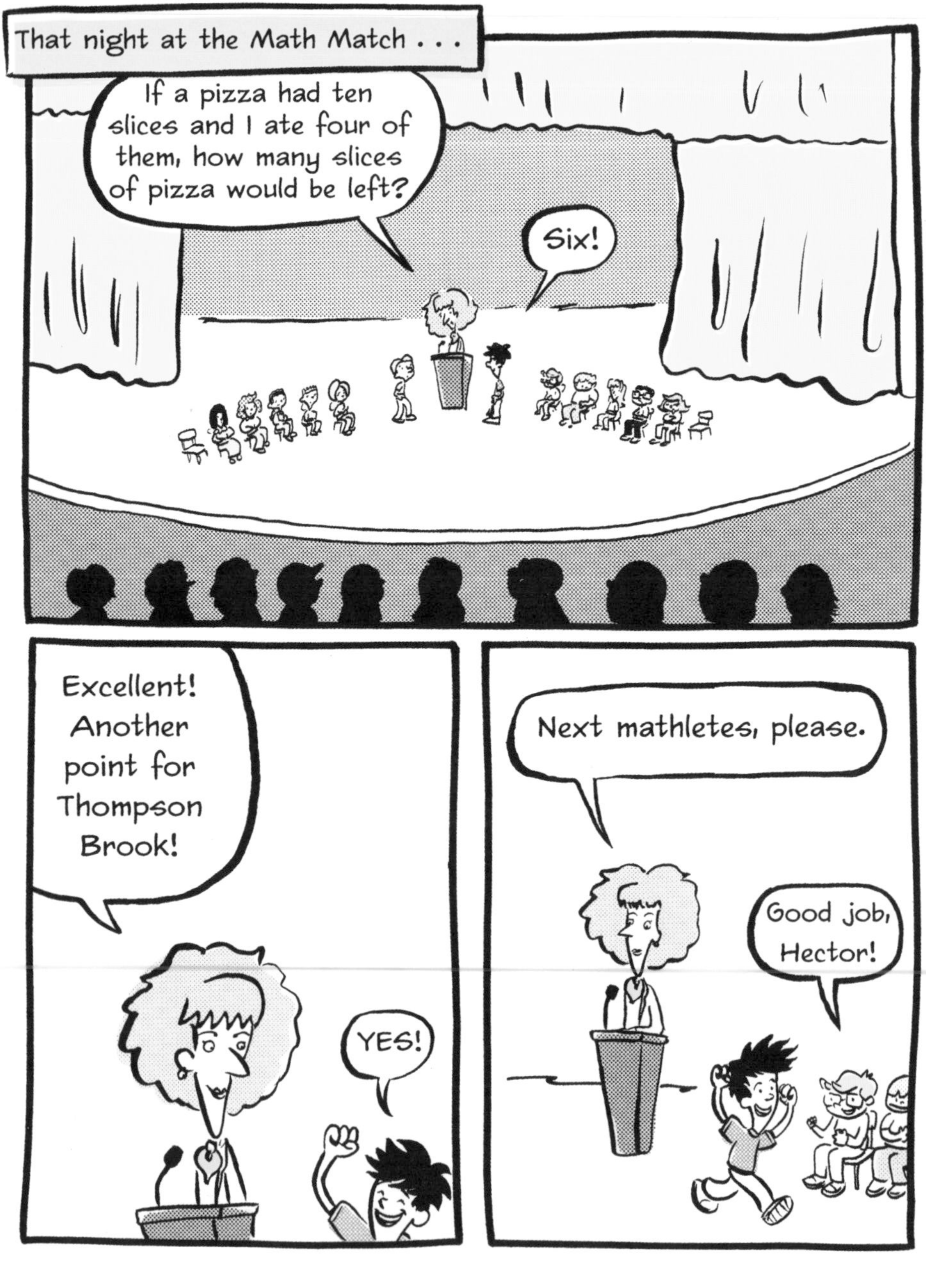
That night at the Math Match . . .
If a pizza had ten slices and I ate four of them, how many slices of pizza would be left?
Six!
Excellent! Another point for Thompson Brook!
YES!
Next mathletes, please.
Good job, Hector!

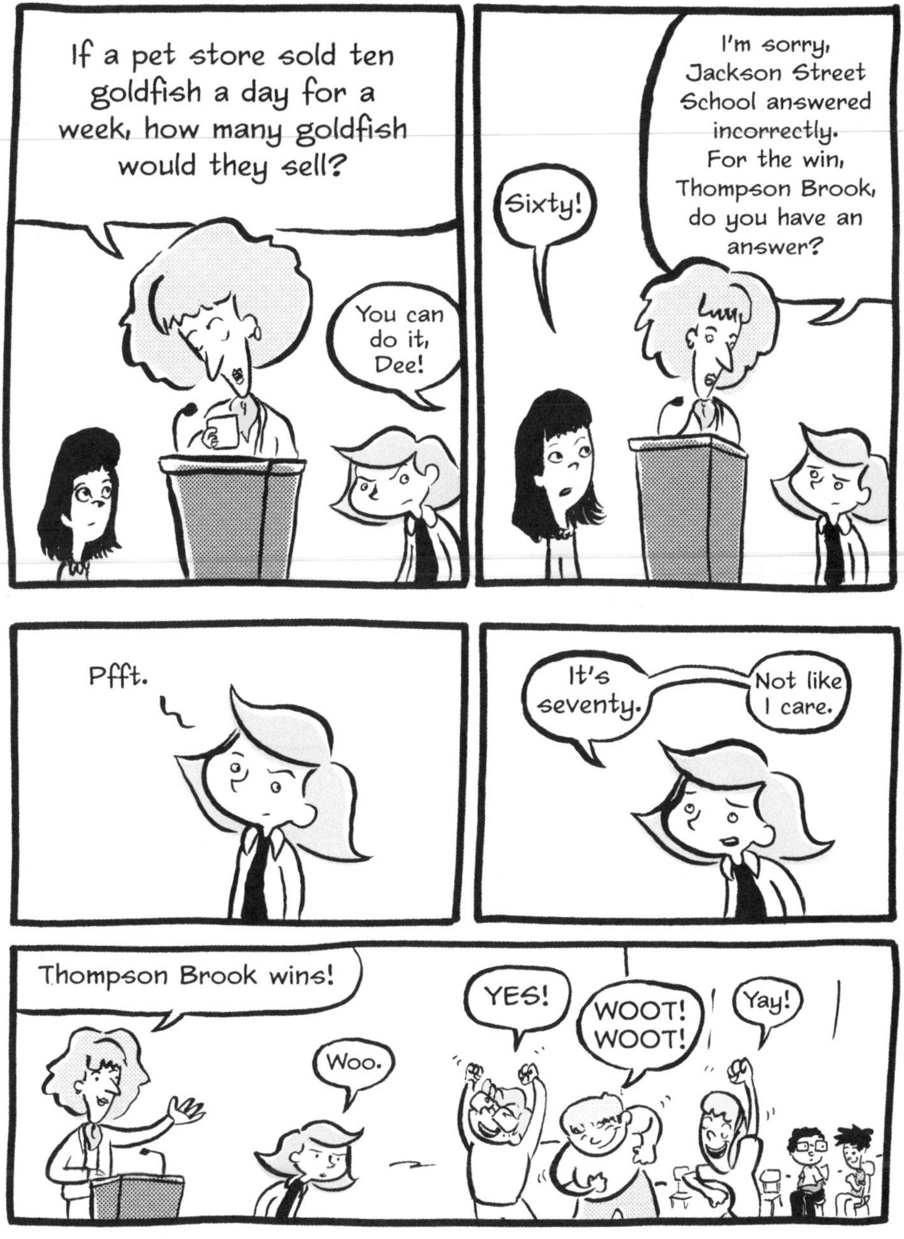

If a pet store sold ten goldfish a day for a week, how many goldfish would they sell?
You can do it, Dee!
Sixty!
I'm sorry, Jackson Street School answered incorrectly. For the win, Thompson Brook, do you have an answer?
Pfft.
It's seventy.
Not like I care.
Thompson Brook wins!
Woo.
YES!
WOOT! WOOT!
Yay!

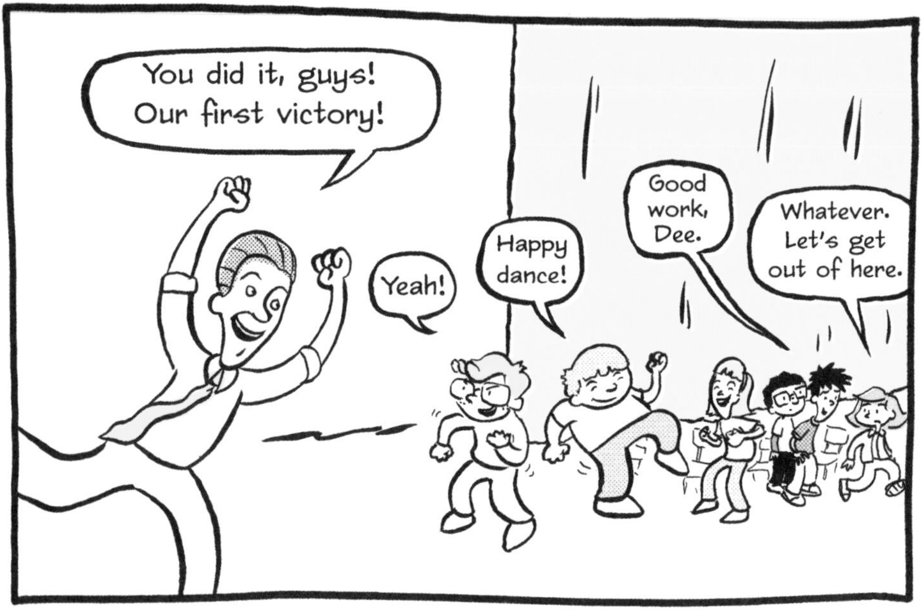
You did it, guys! Our first victory!
Yeah!
Happy dance!
Good work, Dee.
Whatever. Let's get out of here.

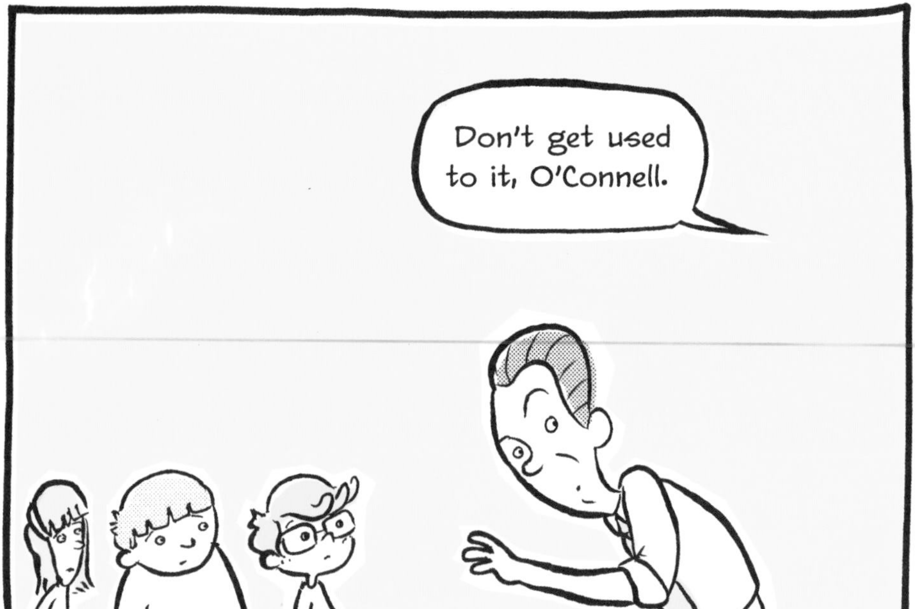
Don't get used to it, O'Connell.

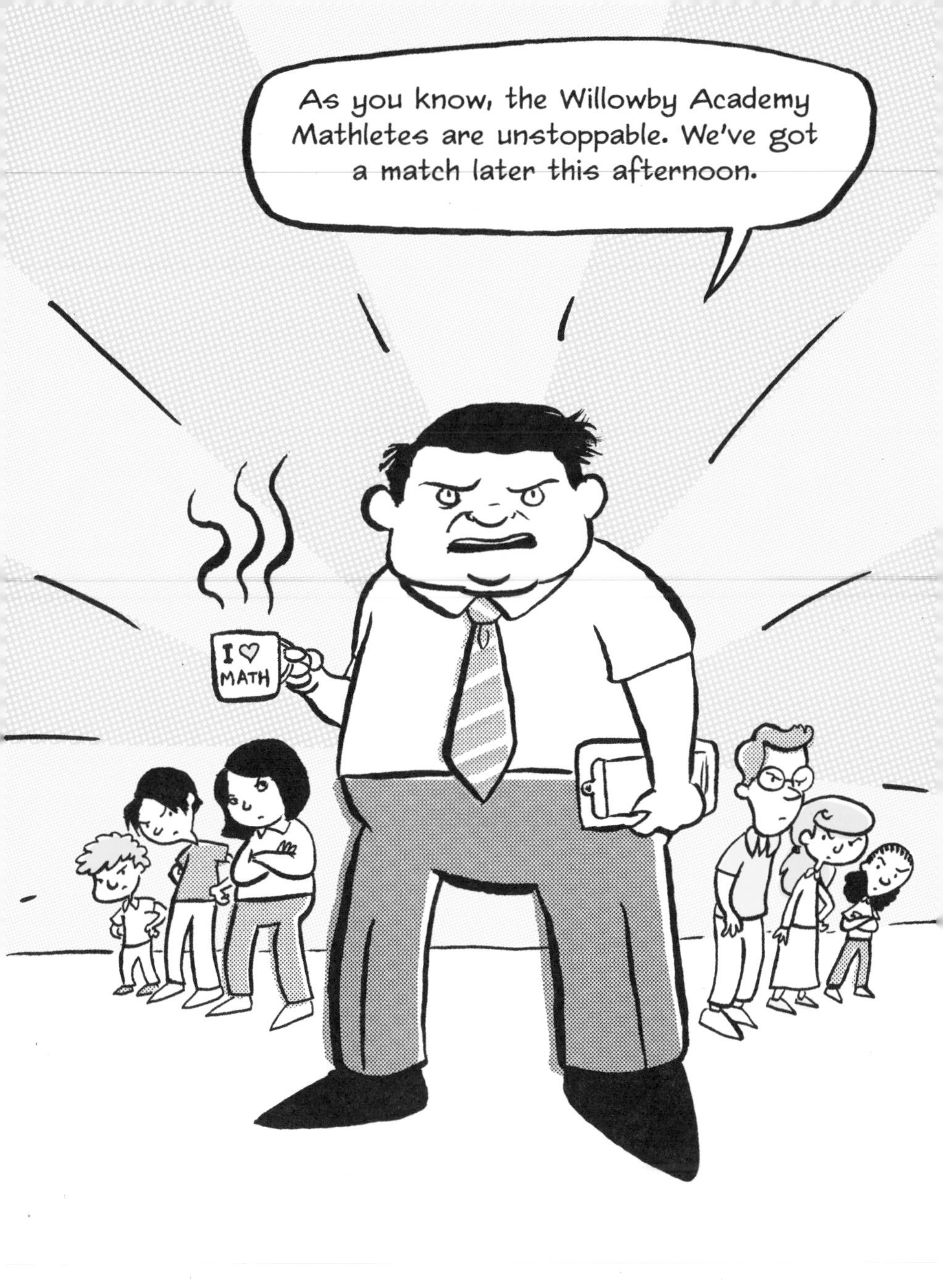
As you know, the Willowby Academy Mathletes are unstoppable. We've got a match later this afternoon.
I ♡ MATH

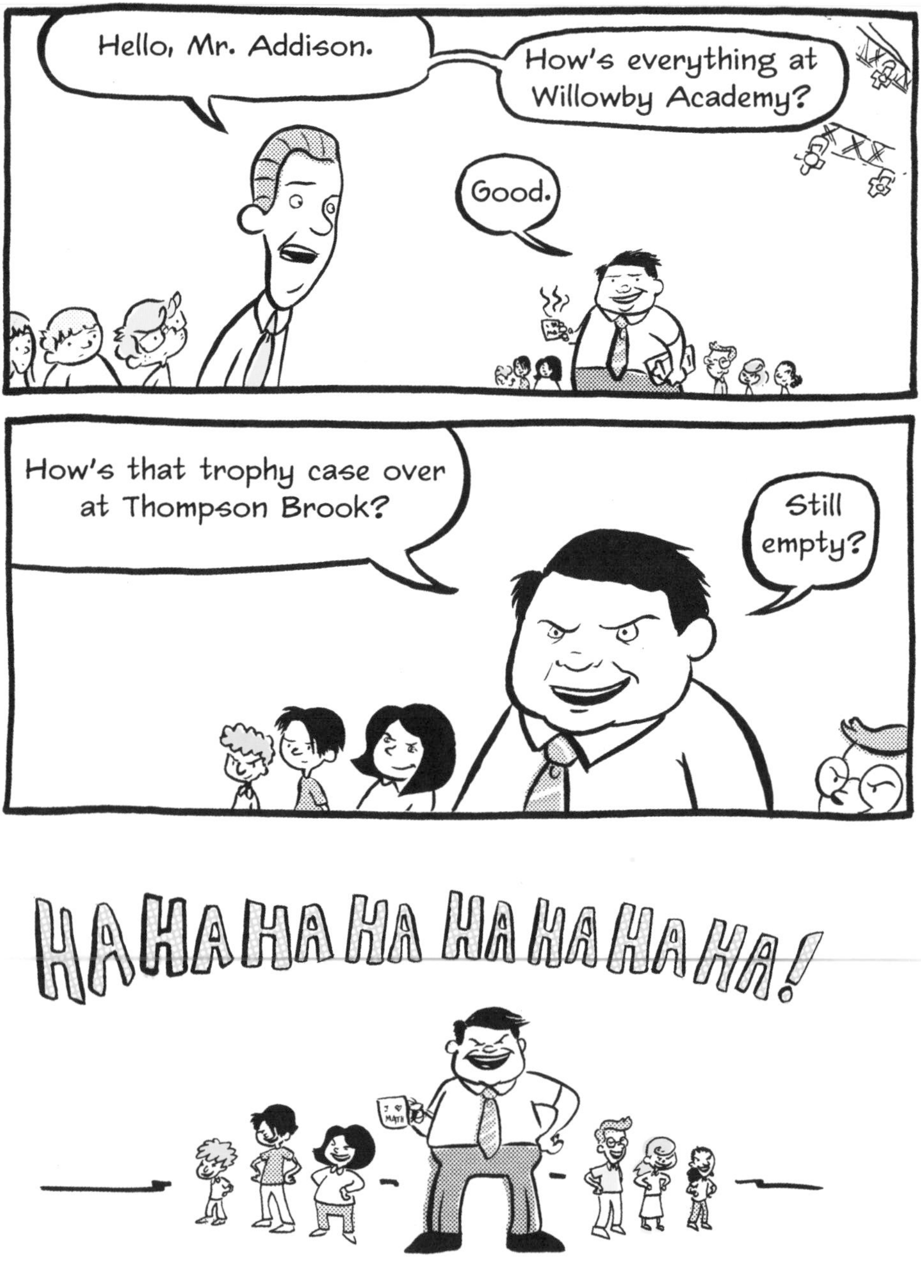
Hello, Mr. Addison.
How's everything at Willowby Academy?
Good.
How's that trophy case over at Thompson Brook?
Still empty?
HAHAHAHAHA HAHAHAHAHA!
I ♥ MATH

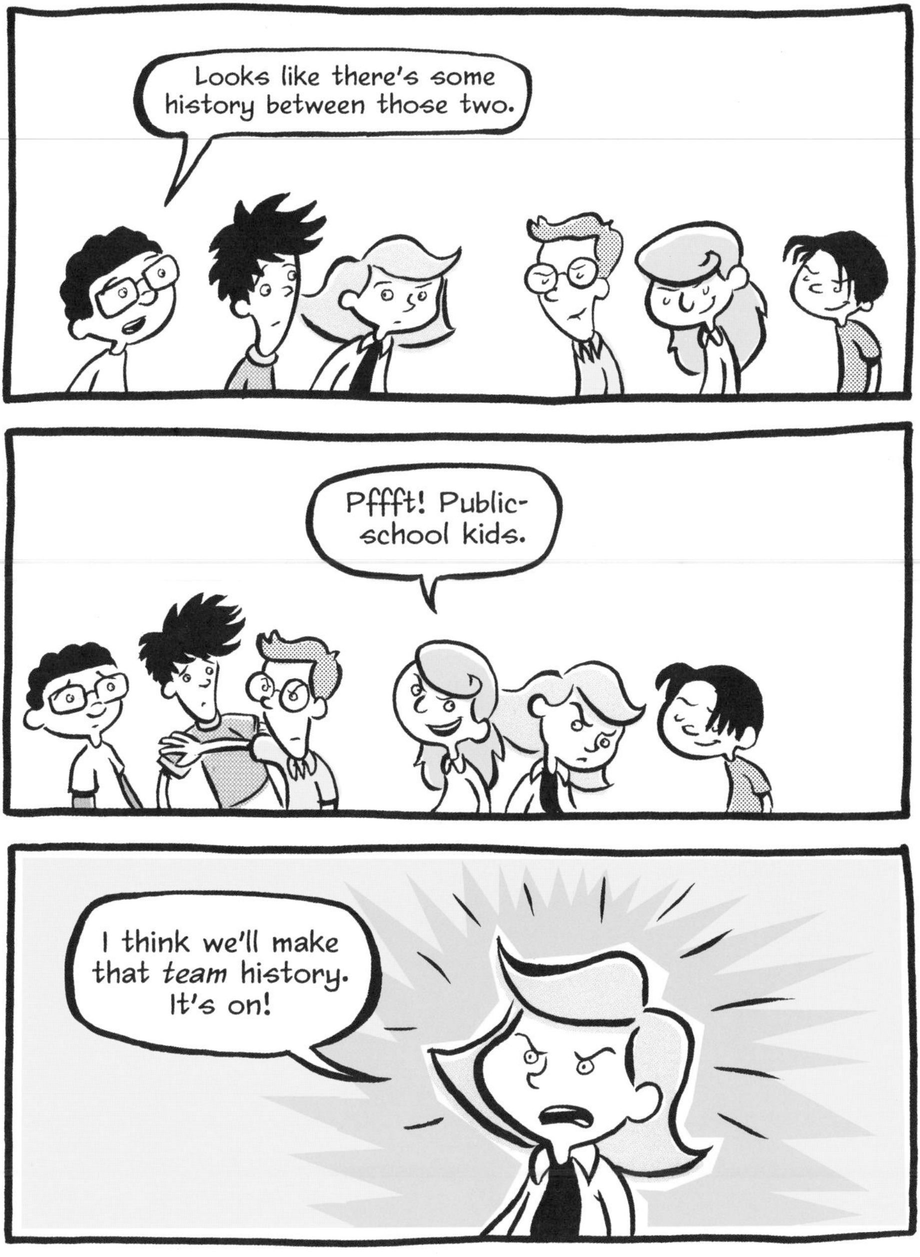
Looks like there's some history between those two.
Pffft! Public-school kids.
I think we'll make that *team* history. It's on!

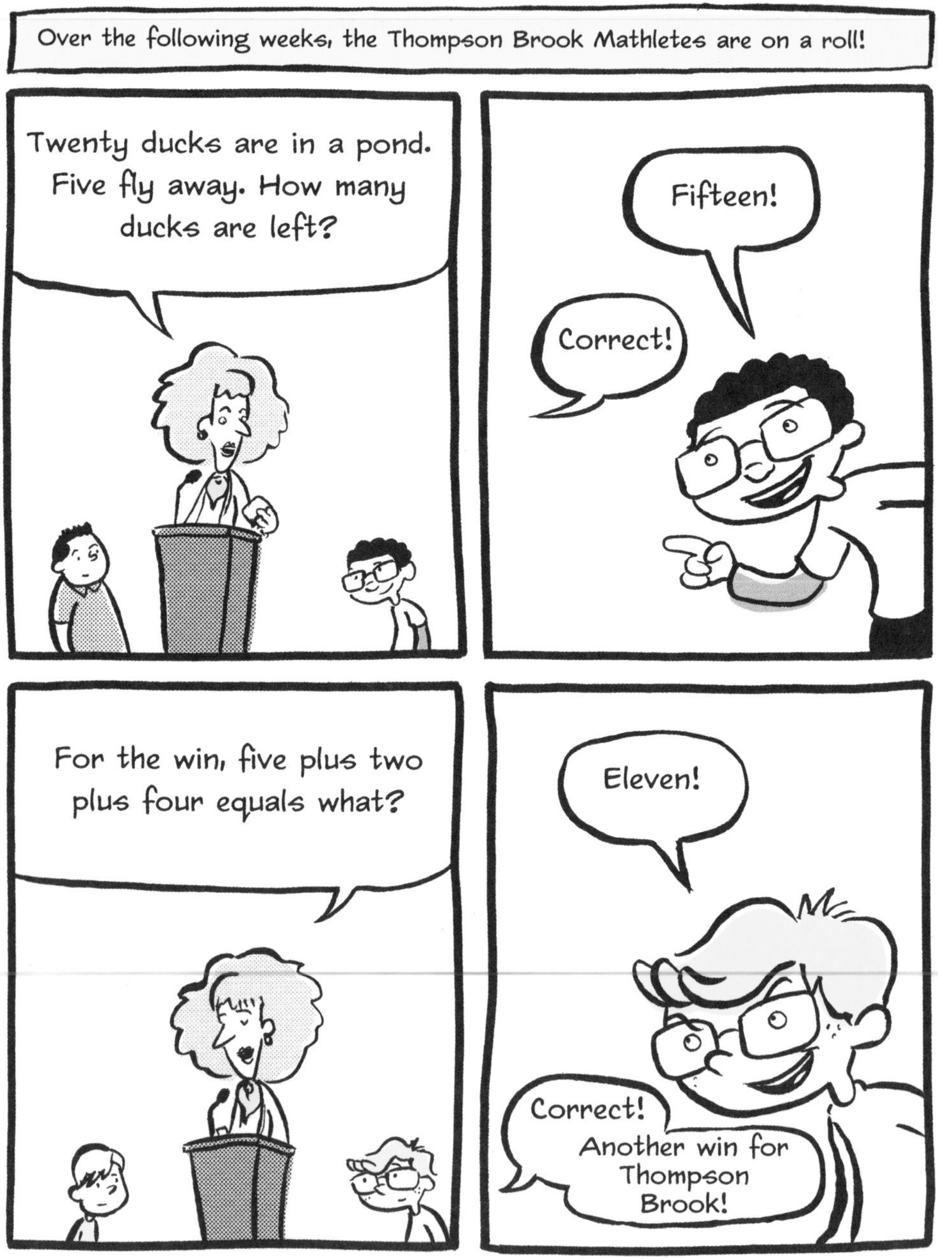
Over the following weeks, the Thompson Brook Mathletes are on a roll!
Twenty ducks are in a pond. Five fly away. How many ducks are left?
Fifteen!
Correct!
For the win, five plus two plus four equals what?
Eleven!
Correct!
Another win for Thompson Brook!

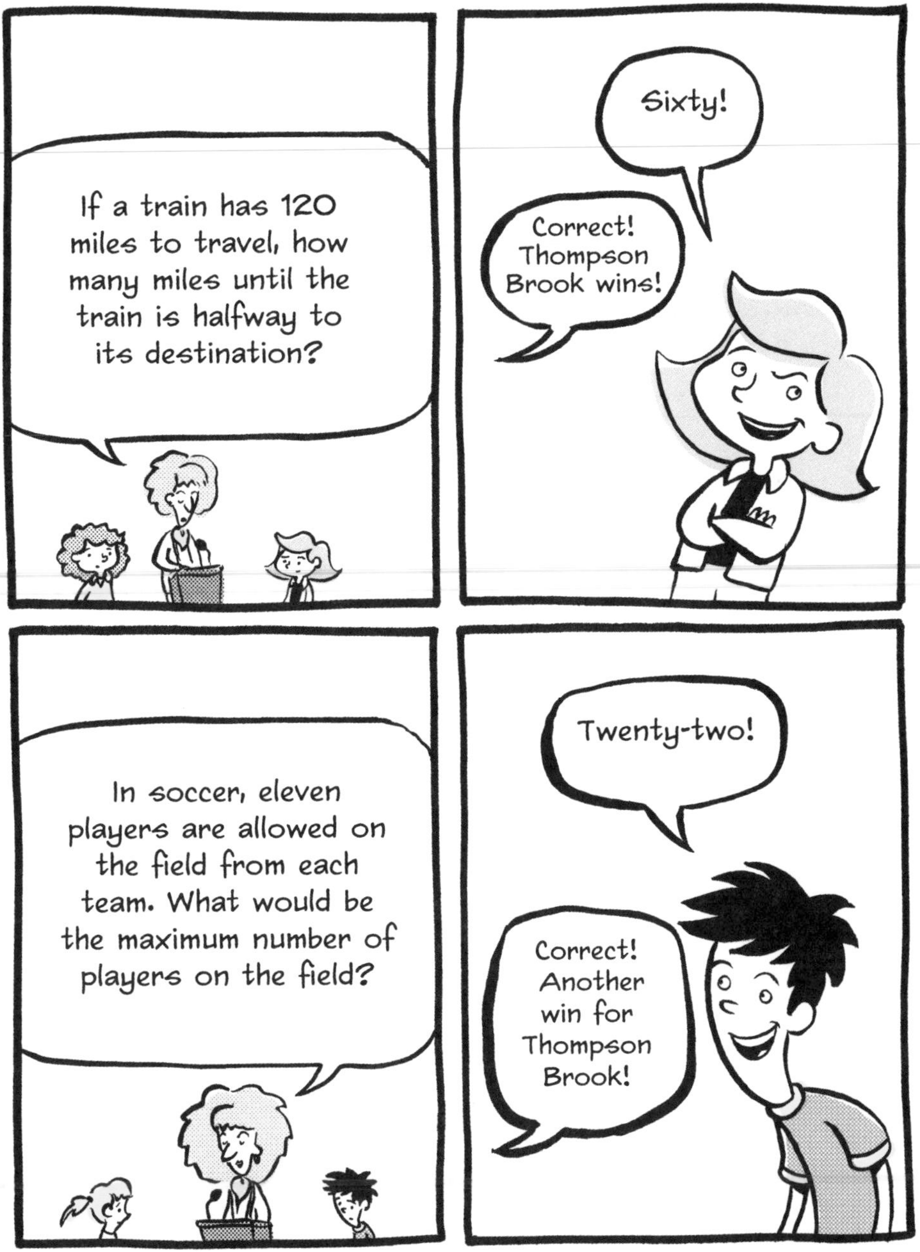
If a train has 120 miles to travel, how many miles until the train is halfway to its destination?
Sixty!
Correct! Thompson Brook wins!
In soccer, eleven players are allowed on the field from each team. What would be the maximum number of players on the field?
Twenty-two!
Correct! Another win for Thompson Brook!

At lunch . . .
Extra fish sticks for the mathletes!
Thanks, Lunch Lady!
You'll need the brainpower for tonight's Math Match!
It's the semifinals! The winner goes on to the Math Bowl!

Gravy?
On fish sticks?!

Gravy?
That's my boy!
You know it, Betty!
Hector, you are sick!

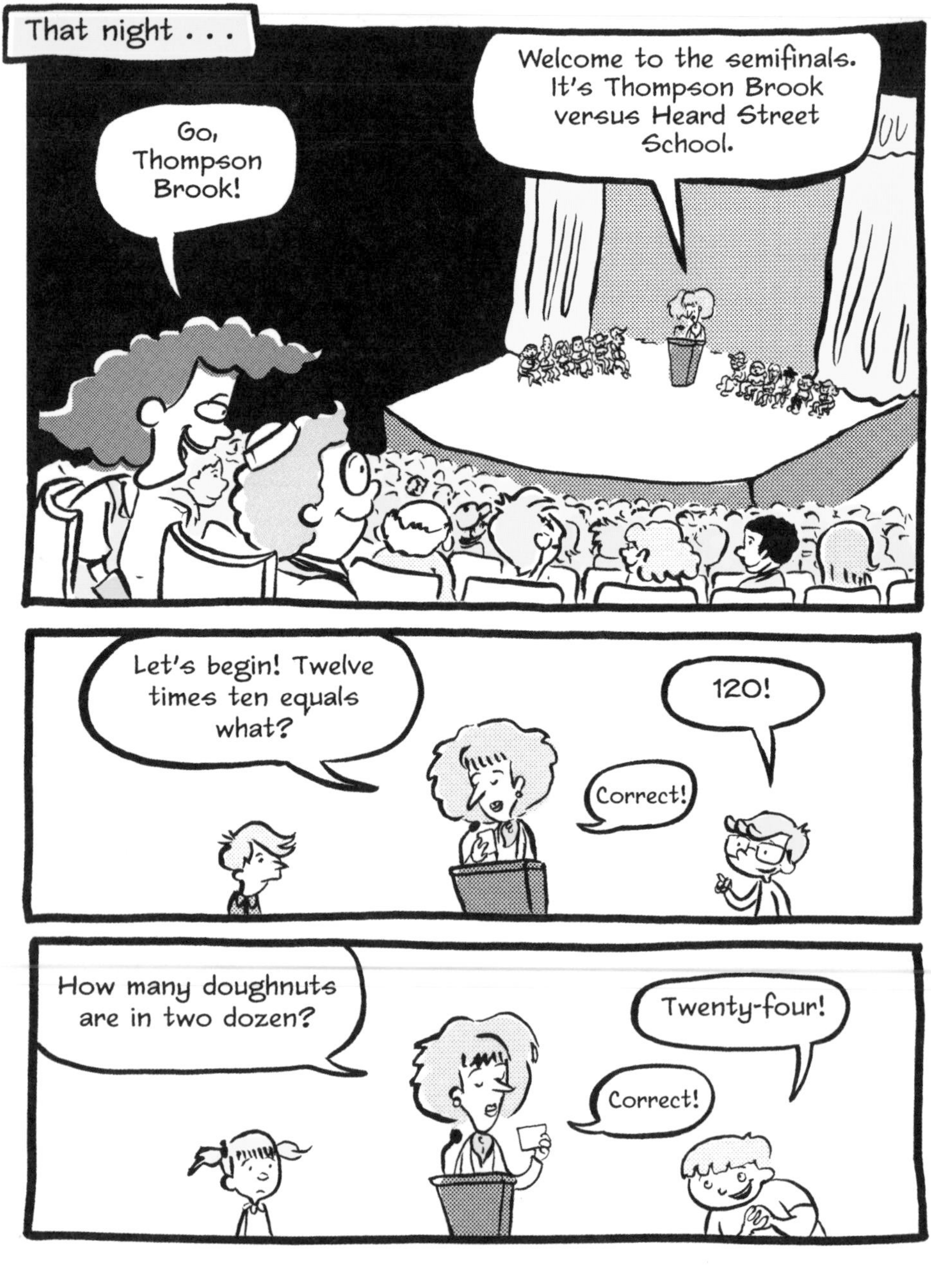
That night . . .
Go, Thompson Brook!
Welcome to the semifinals. It's Thompson Brook versus Heard Street School.
Let's begin! Twelve times ten equals what?
120!
Correct!
How many doughnuts are in two dozen?
Twenty-four!
Correct!

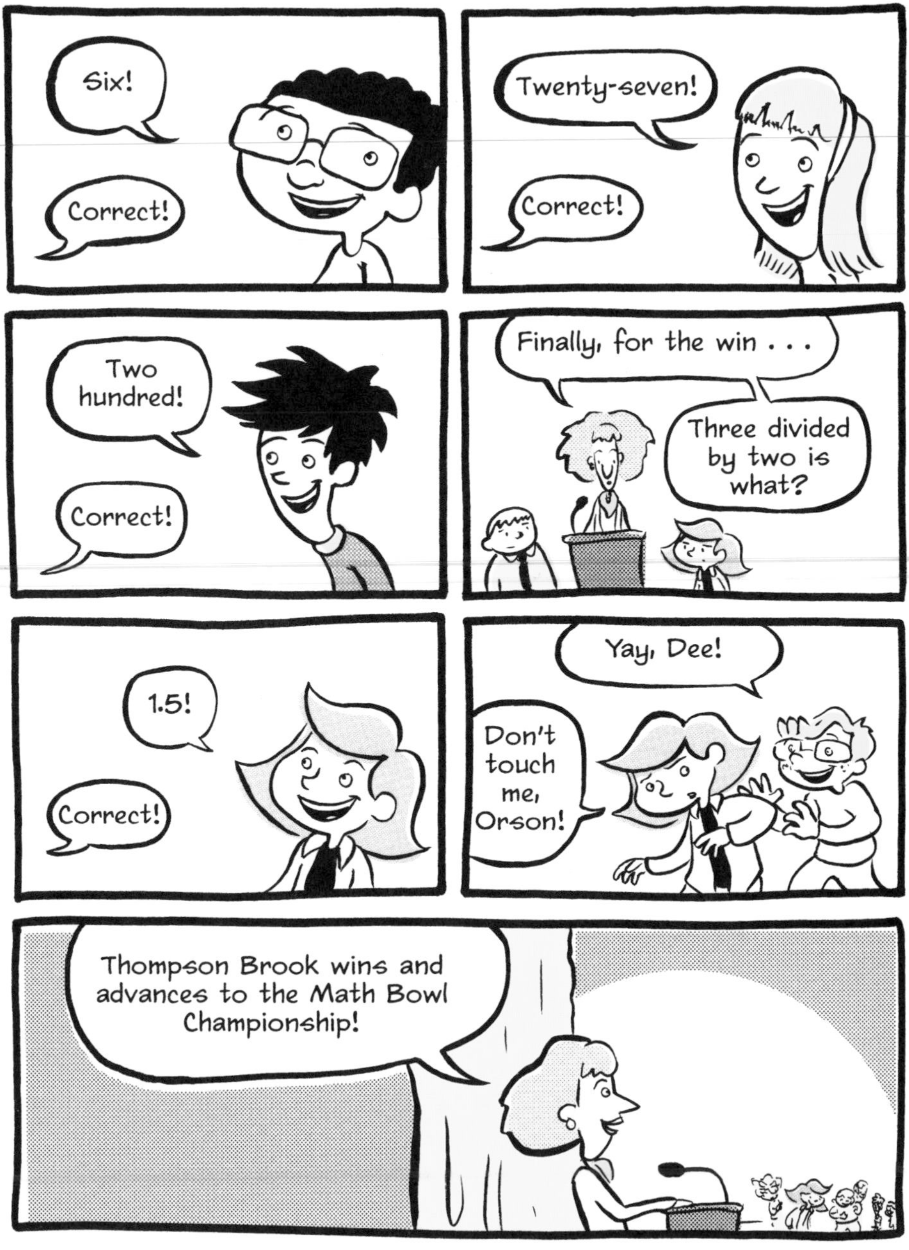
Six!
Correct!
Twenty-seven!
Correct!
Two hundred!
Correct!
Finally, for the win . . .
Three divided by two is what?
1.5!
Correct!
Yay, Dee!
Don't touch me, Orson!
Thompson Brook wins and advances to the Math Bowl Championship!

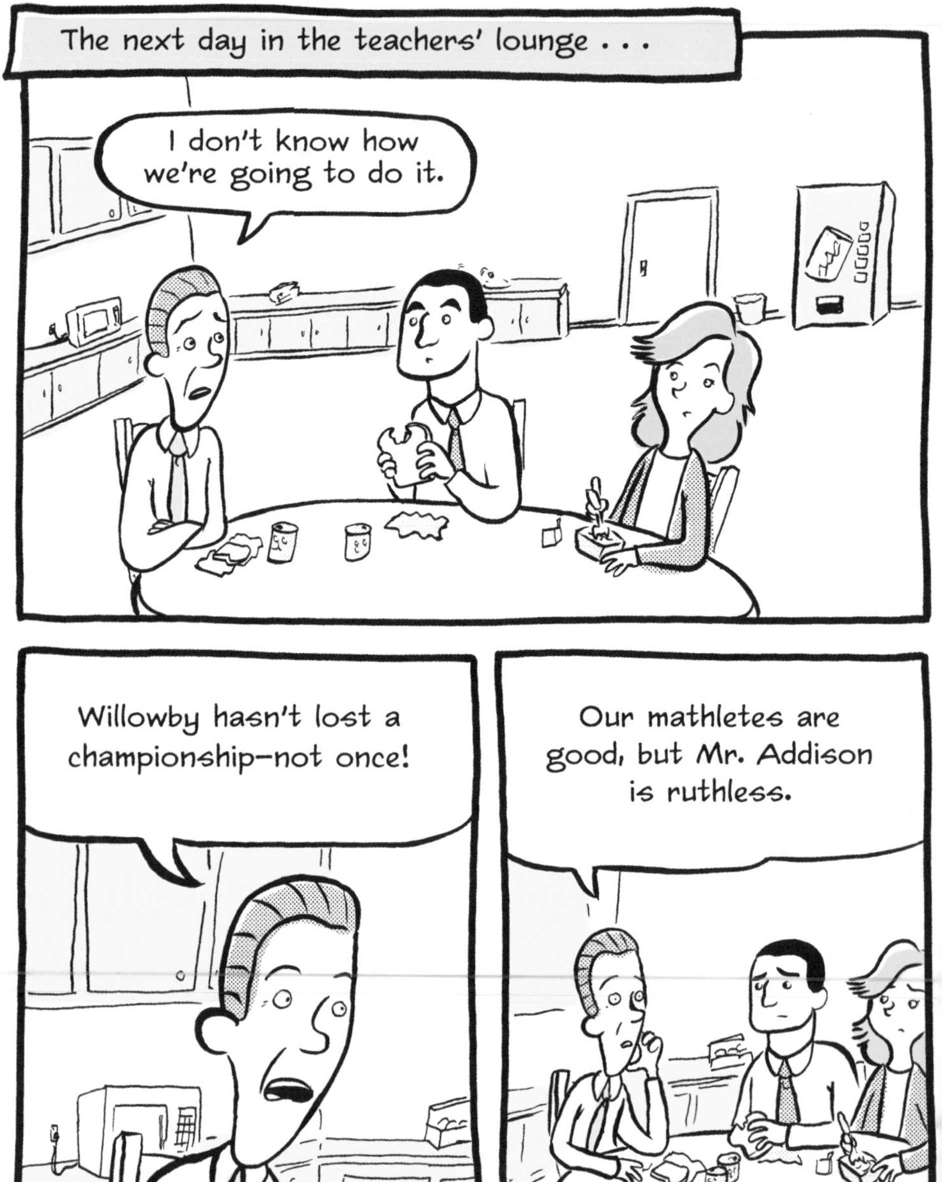
The next day in the teachers' lounge . . .
I don't know how we're going to do it.
Willowby hasn't lost a championship–not once!
Our mathletes are good, but Mr. Addison is ruthless.

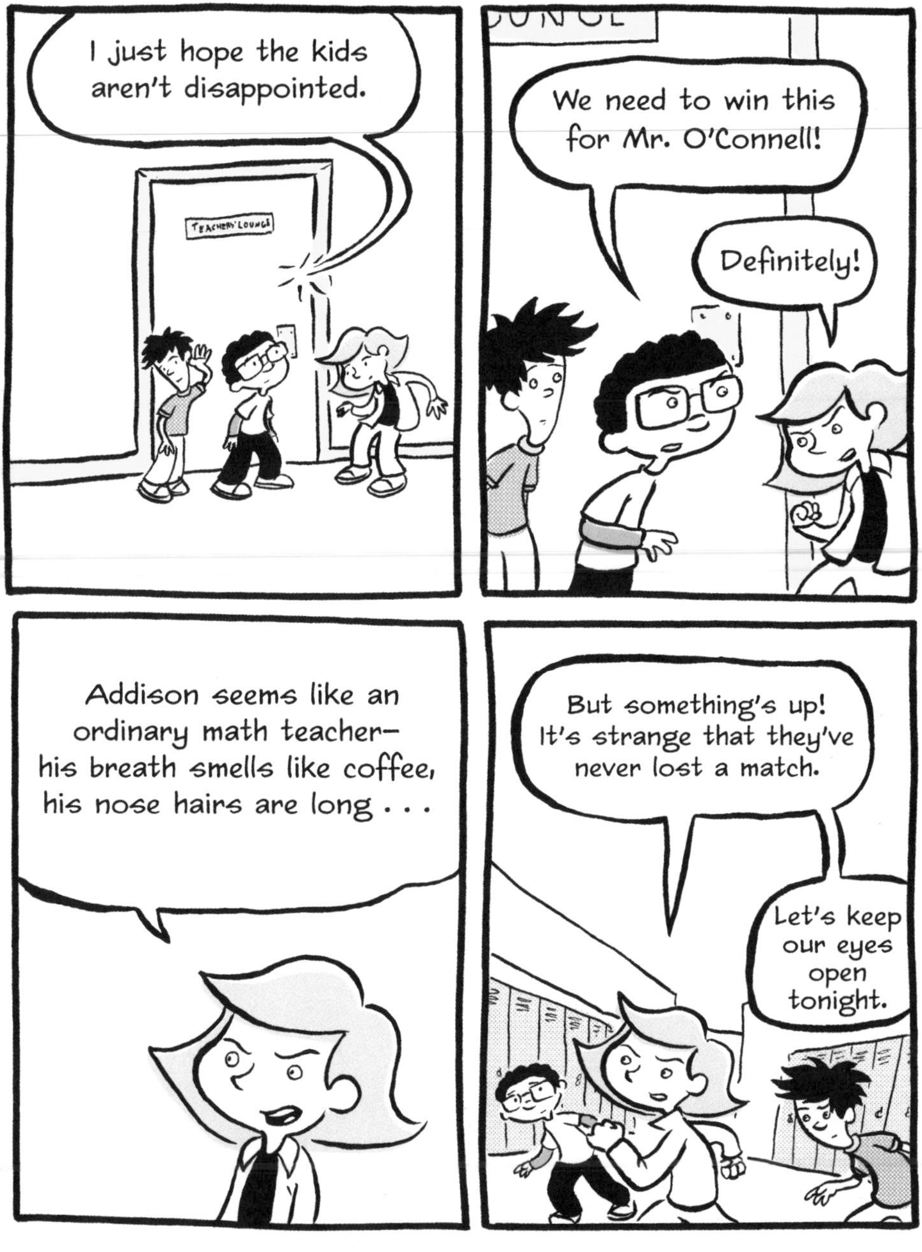
I just hope the kids aren't disappointed.
TEACHERS' LOUNGE
We need to win this for Mr. O'Connell!
Definitely!
Addison seems like an ordinary math teacher— his breath smells like coffee, his nose hairs are long . . .
But something's up! It's strange that they've never lost a match.
Let's keep our eyes open tonight.

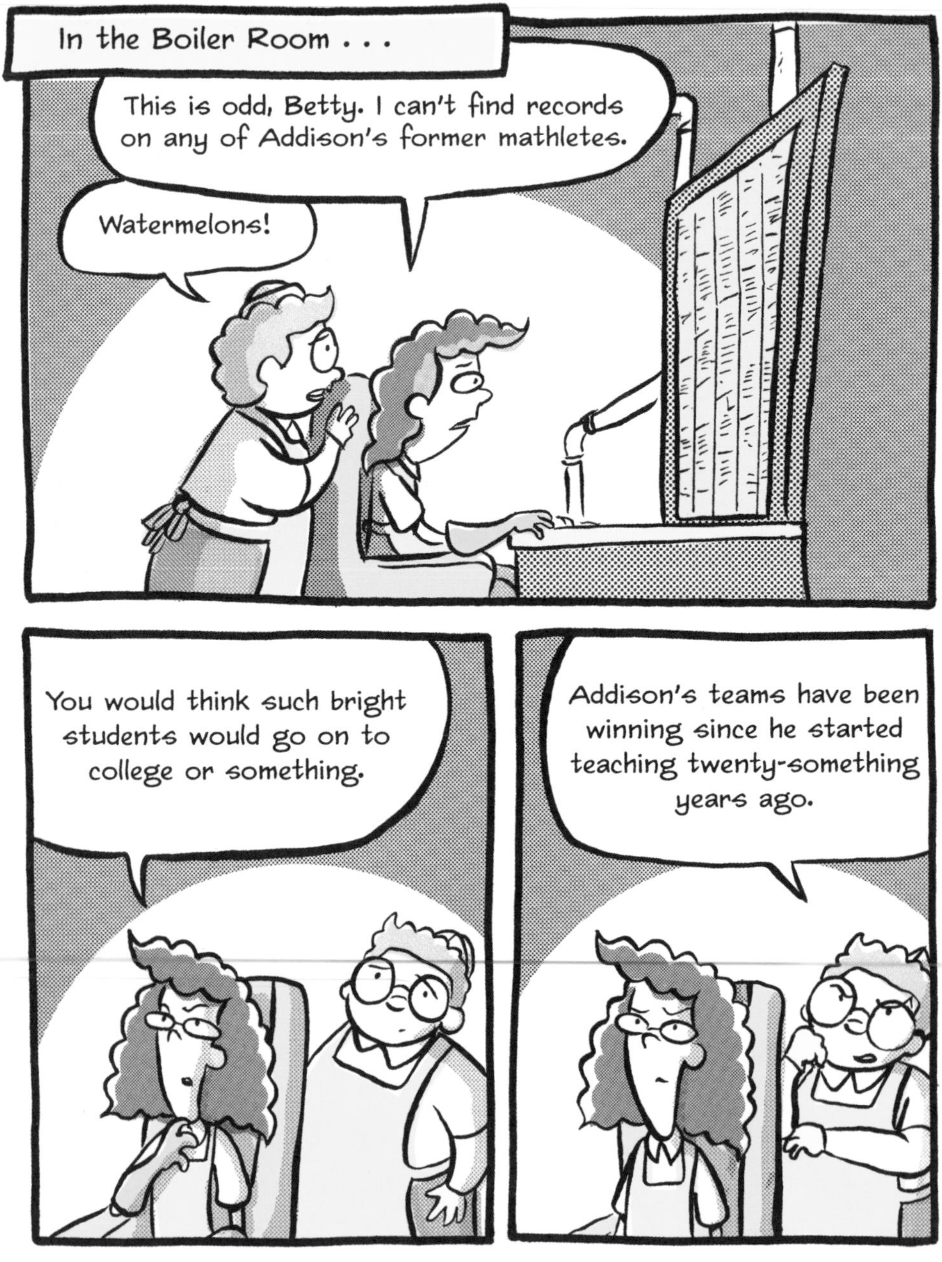
In the Boiler Room . . .
This is odd, Betty. I can't find records on any of Addison's former mathletes.
Watermelons!
You would think such bright students would go on to college or something.
Addison's teams have been winning since he started teaching twenty-something years ago.

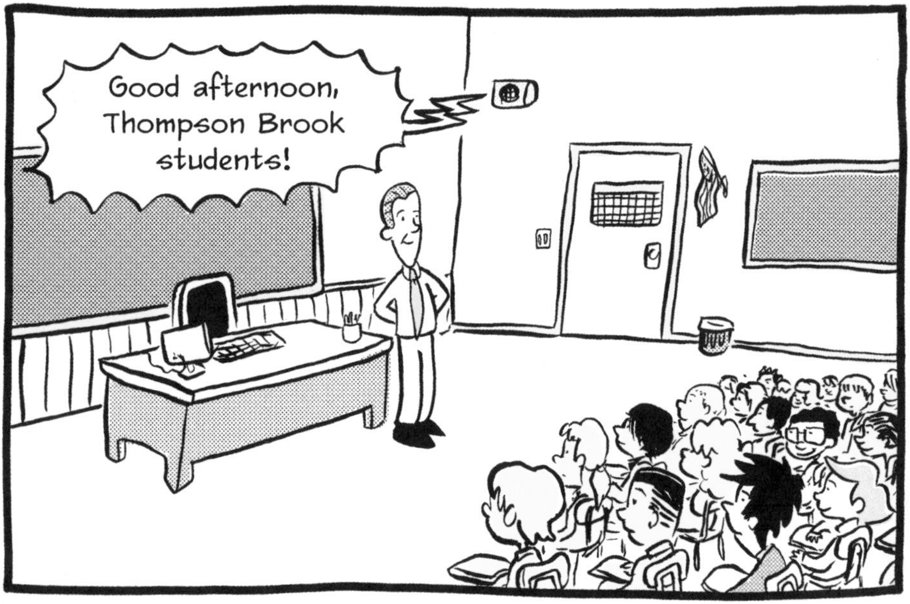
Good afternoon, Thompson Brook students!

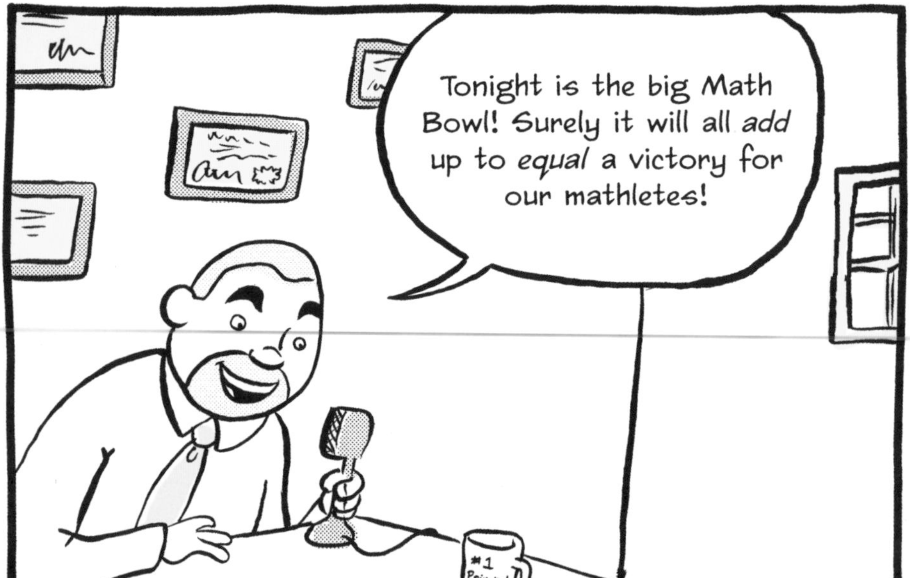
Tonight is the big Math Bowl! Surely it will all add up to equal a victory for our mathletes!
#1 Principal

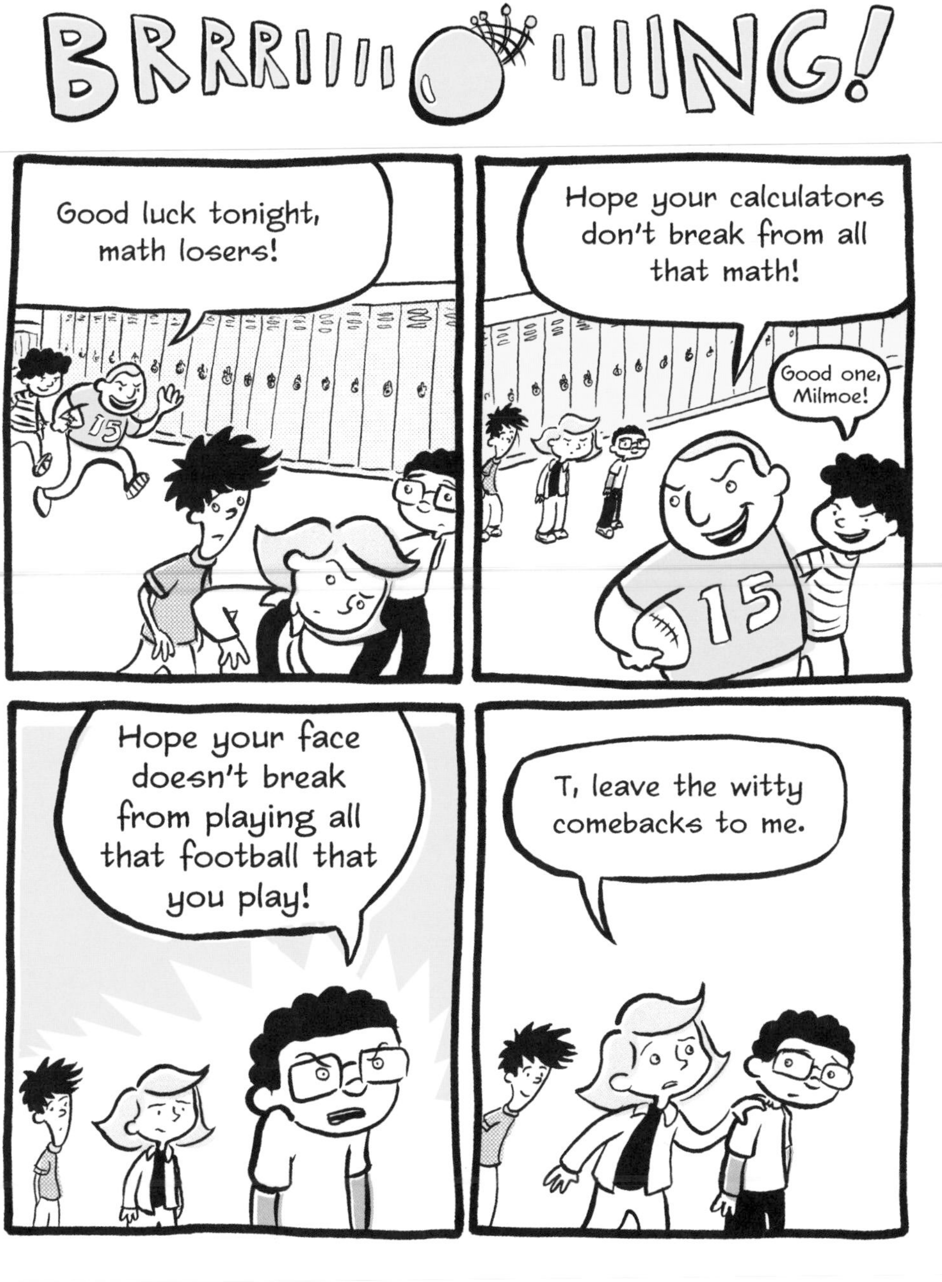
BRRRIIIIIIIIIIING!
Good luck tonight, math losers!
Hope your calculators don't break from all that math!
Good one, Milmoe!
Hope your face doesn't break from playing all that football that you play!
T, leave the witty comebacks to me.

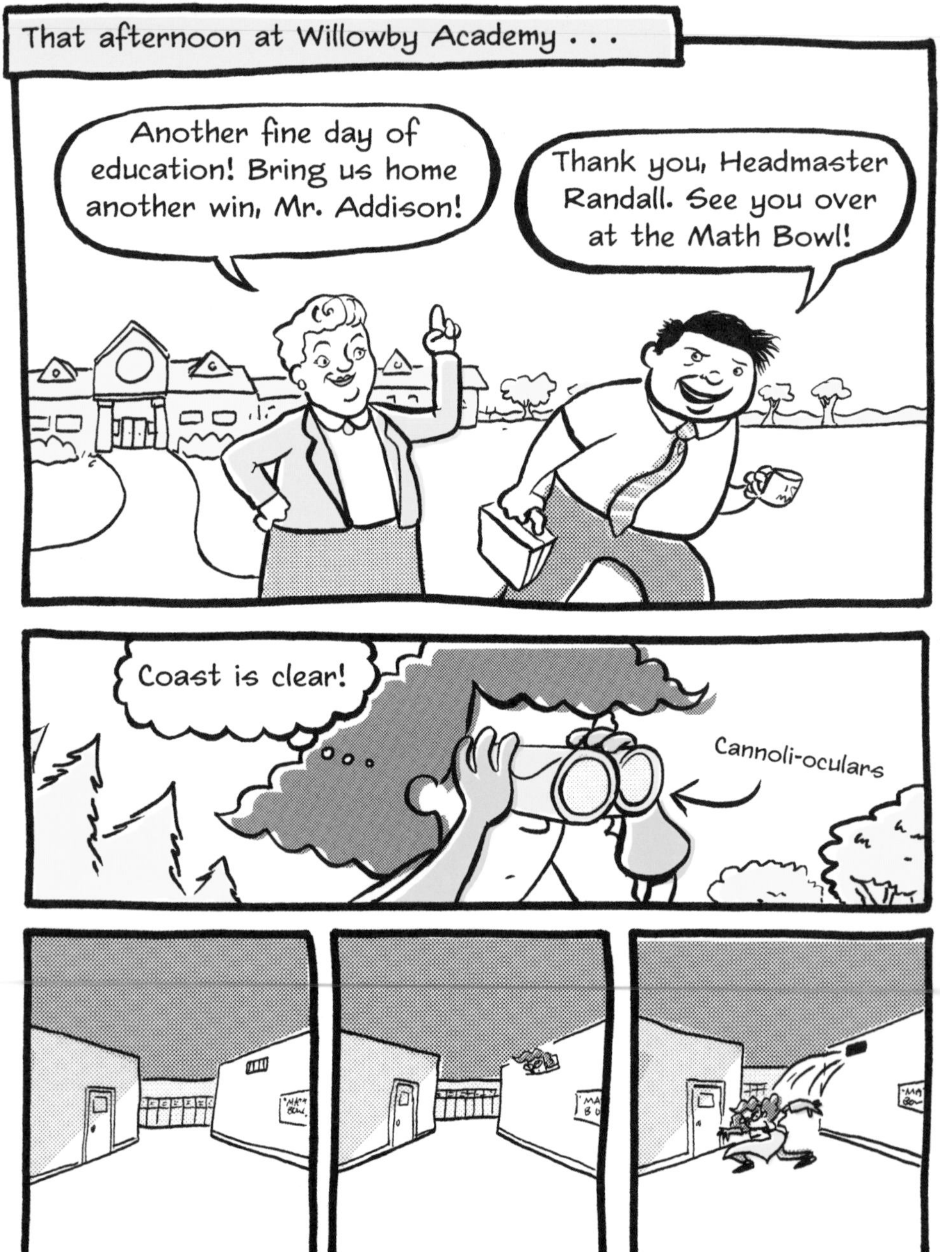
That afternoon at Willowby Academy . . .
Another fine day of education! Bring us home another win, Mr. Addison!
Thank you, Headmaster Randall. See you over at the Math Bowl!
Coast is clear!
Cannoli-oculars

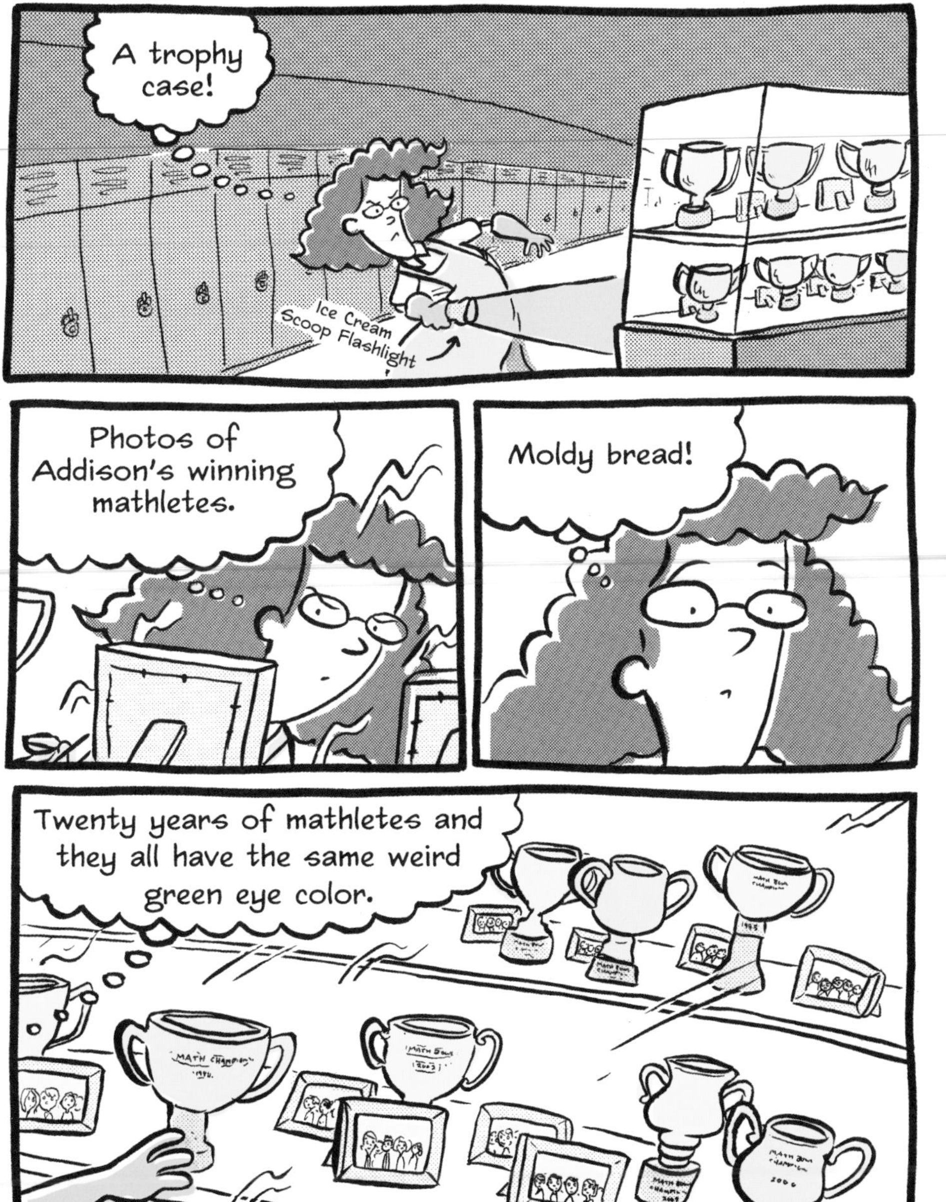
A trophy case!
Ice Cream Scoop Flashlight
Photos of Addison's winning mathletes.
Moldy bread!
Twenty years of mathletes and they all have the same weird green eye color.

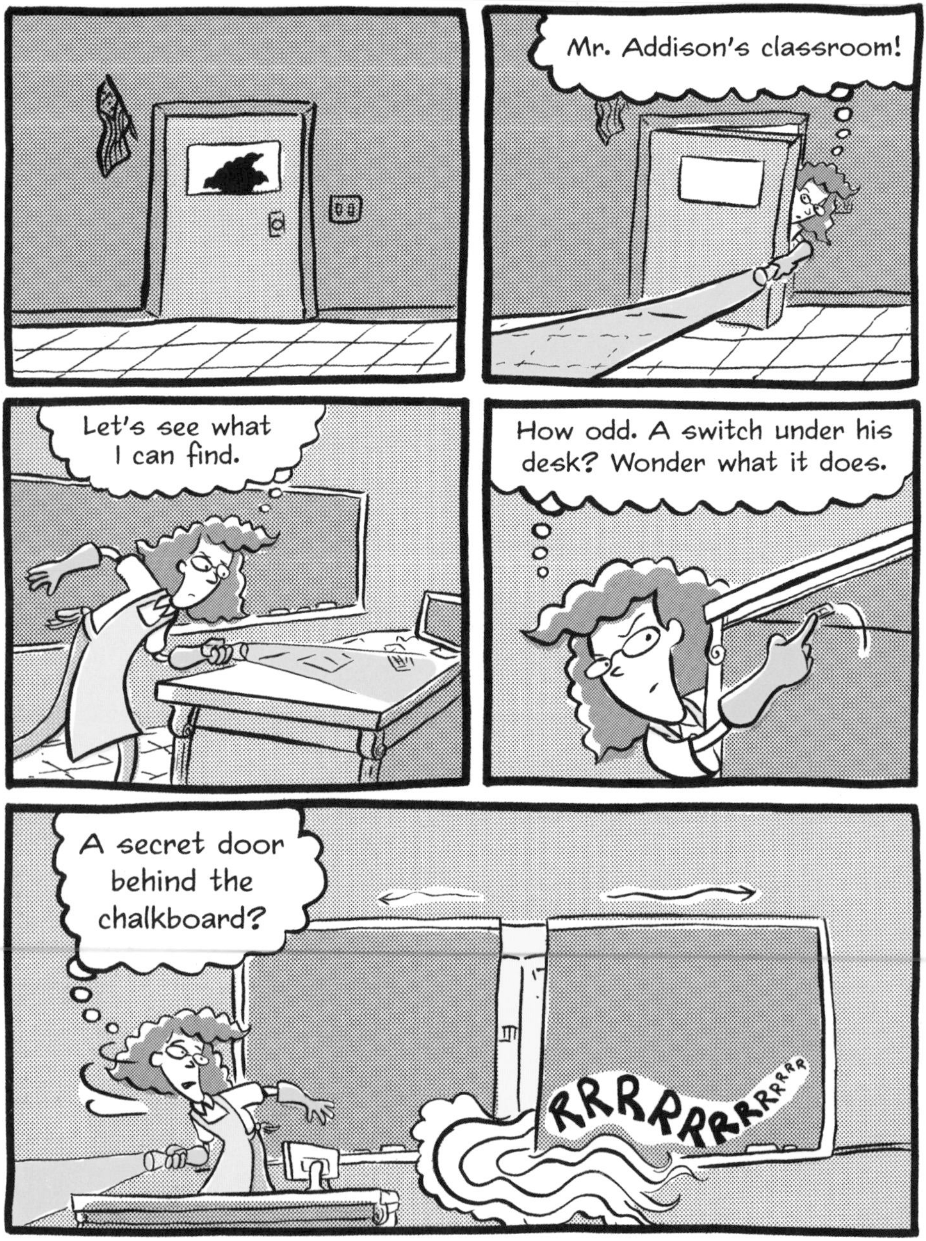
Mr. Addison's classroom!
Let's see what I can find.
How odd. A switch under his desk? Wonder what it does.
A secret door behind the chalkboard?
RRRRRRRRRRRRRRR

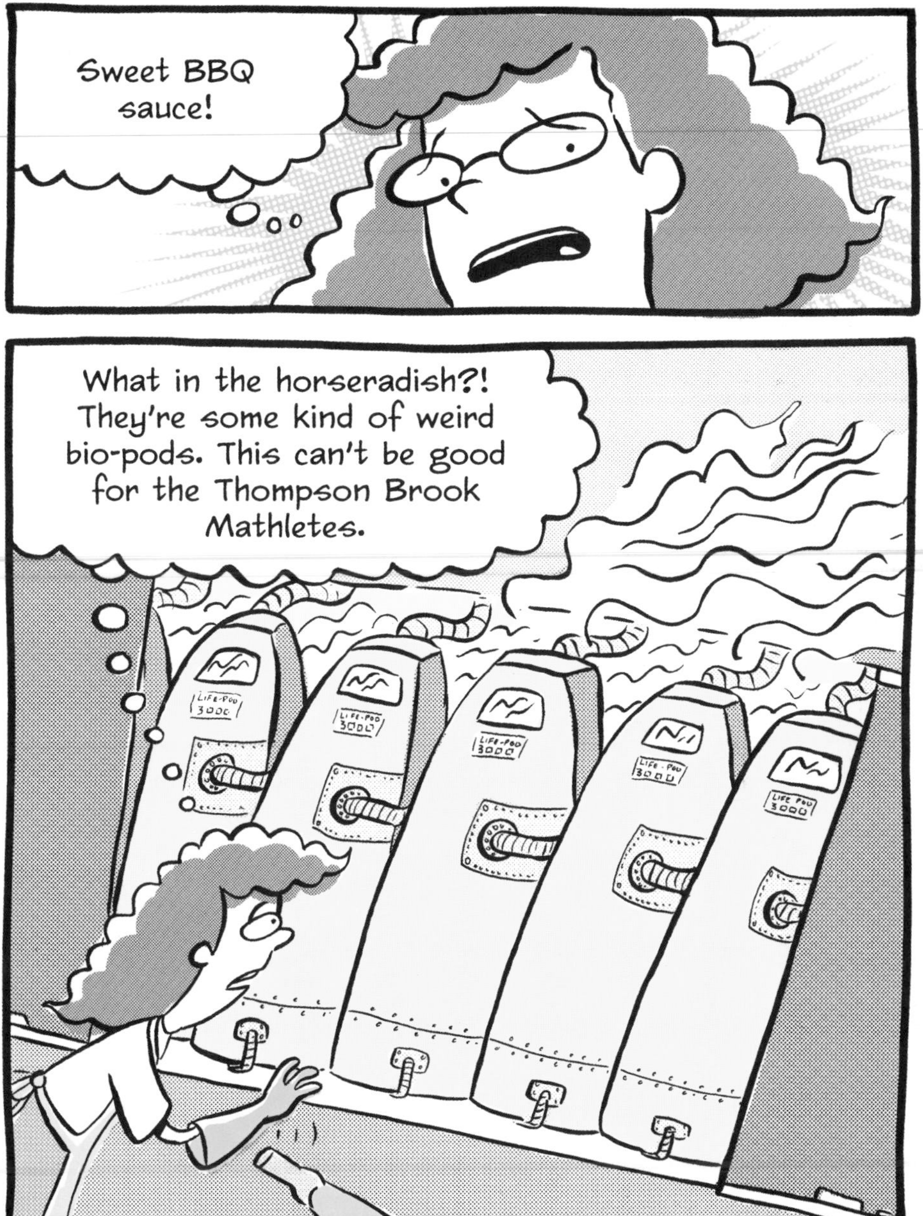
Sweet BBQ sauce!
What in the horseradish?! They're some kind of weird bio-pods. This can't be good for the Thompson Brook Mathletes.

Hey, lady, you're going to regret ever seeing Addison's lab! You know I can't let you leave now, right?
What does this all mean?

It means your mathletes are doomed! We here at Willowby Academy are winners!
OOOOF!

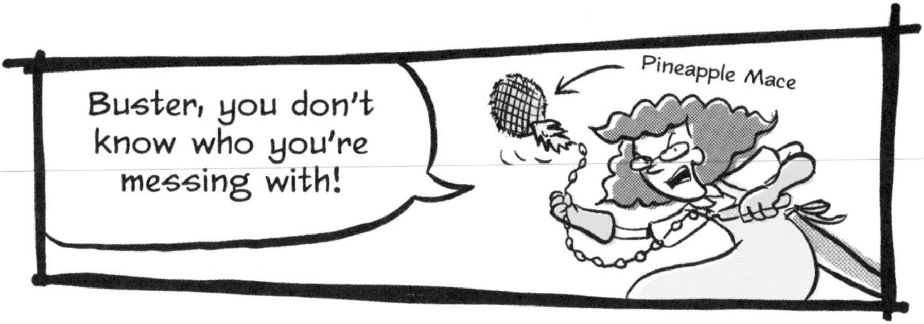
Buster, you don't know who you're messing with!
Pineapple Mace

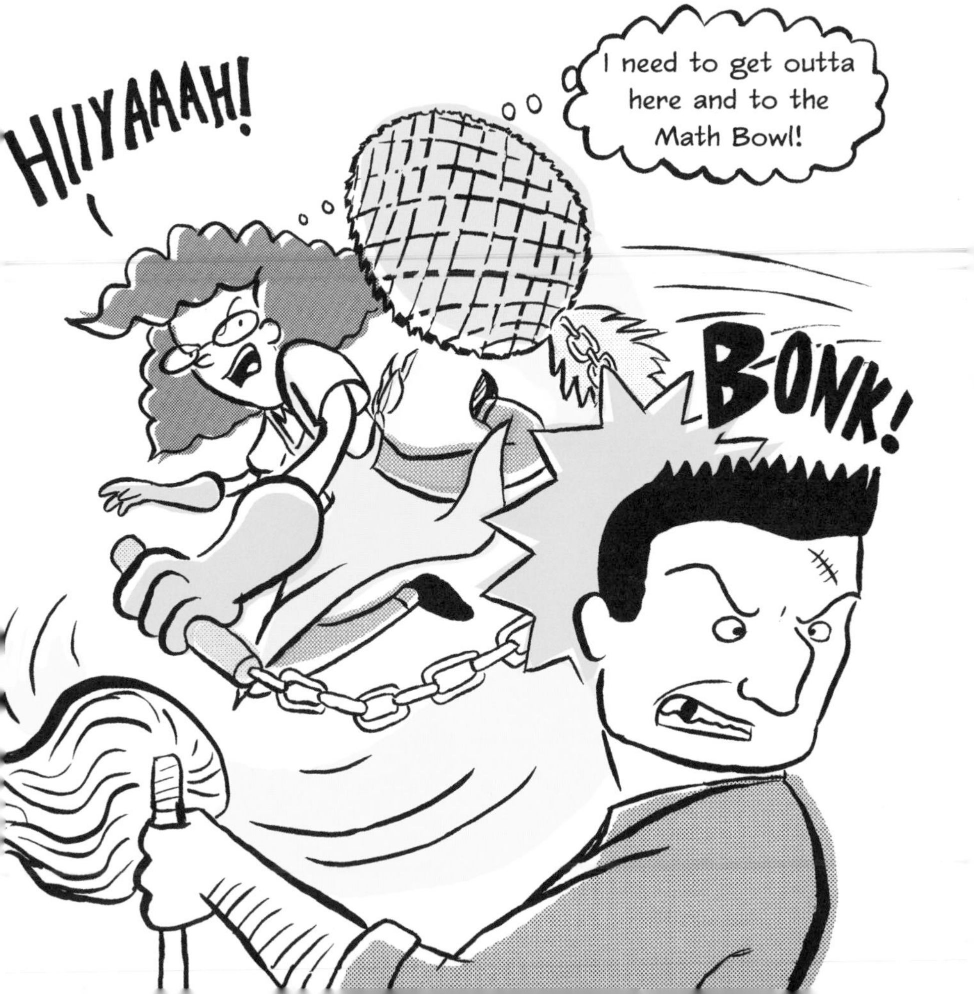
HIIYAAAH!
I need to get outta here and to the Math Bowl!
BONK!

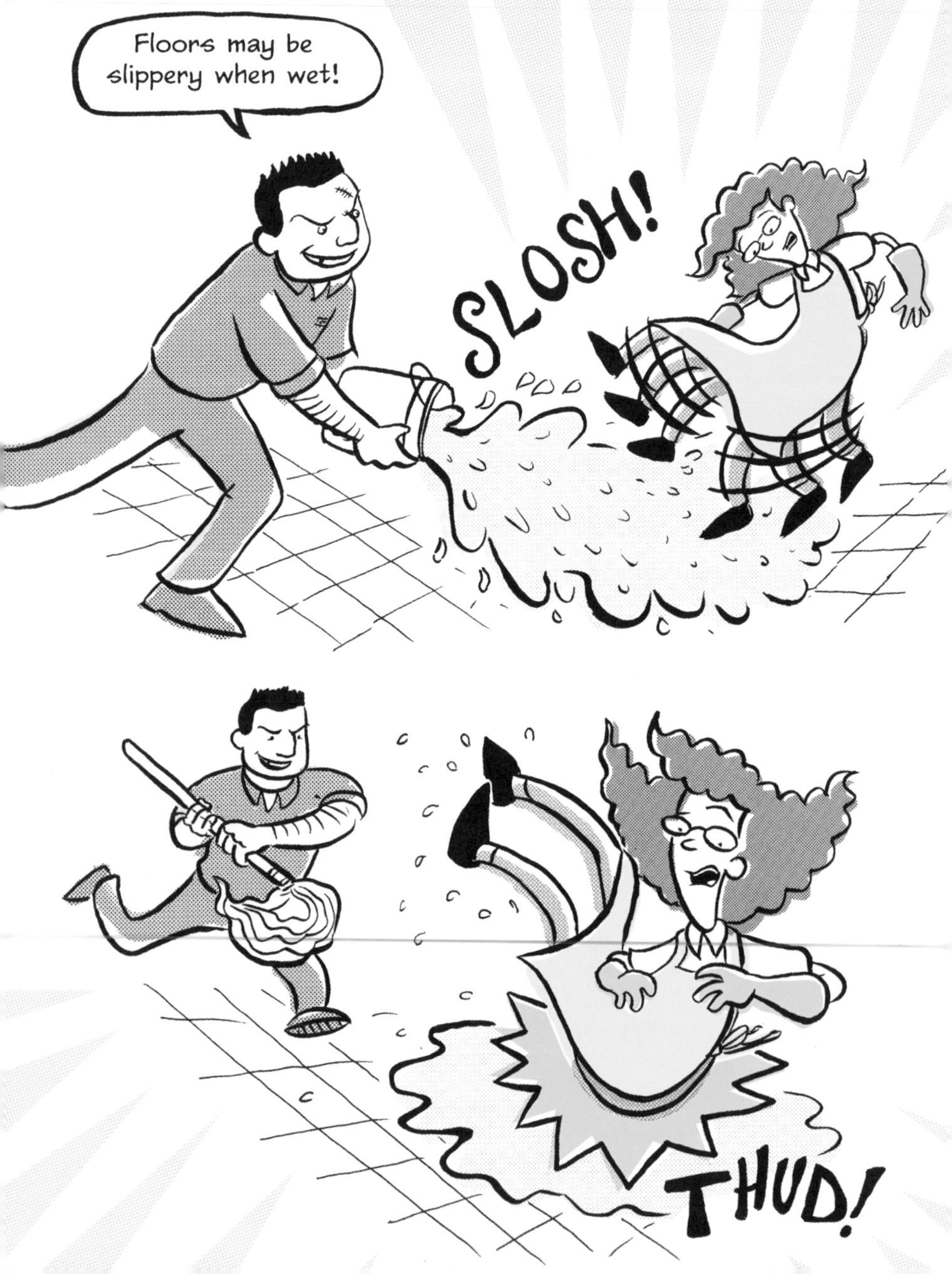
Floors may be slippery when wet!
SLOSH!
THUD!

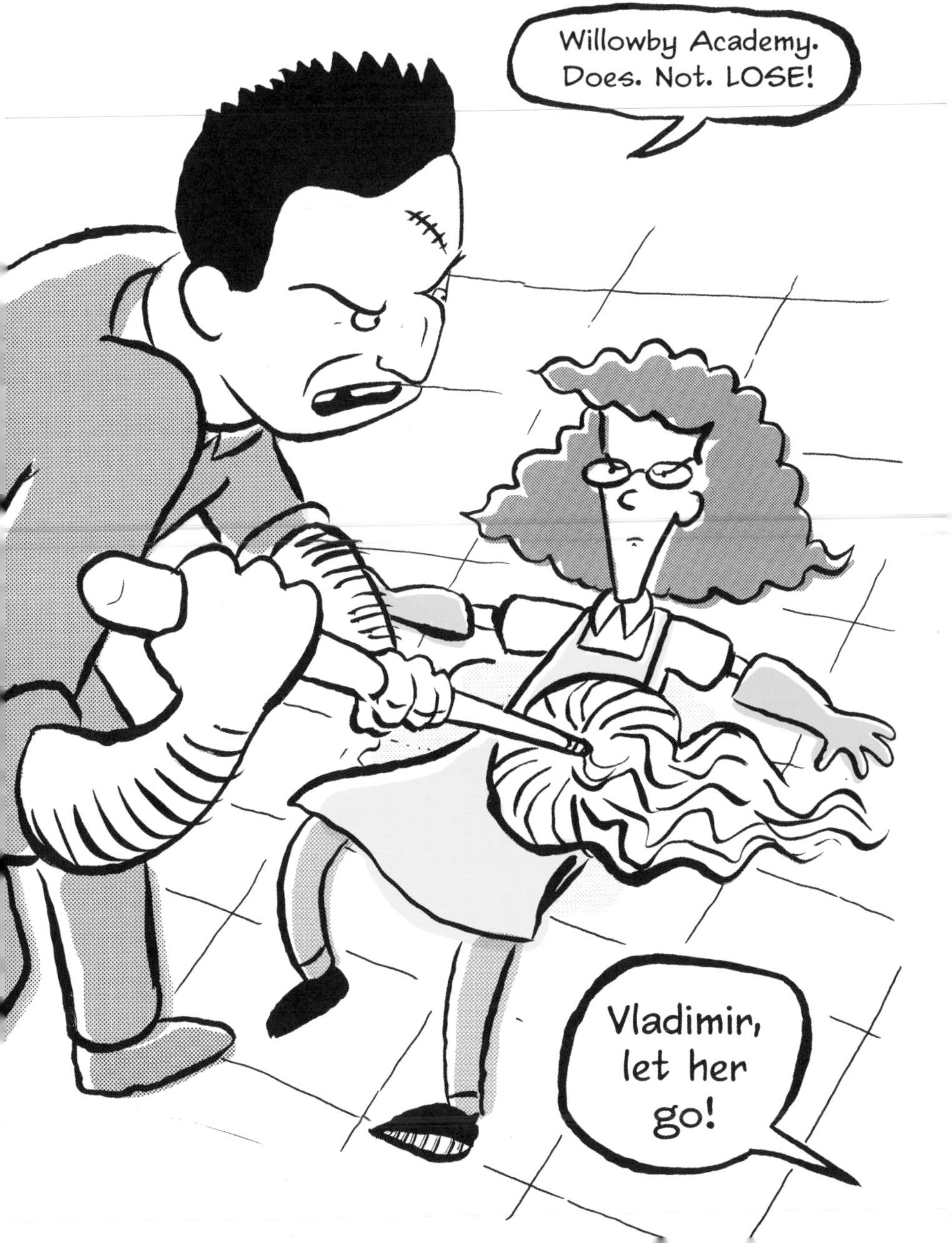
Willowby Academy. Does. Not. LOSE!
Vladimir, let her go!

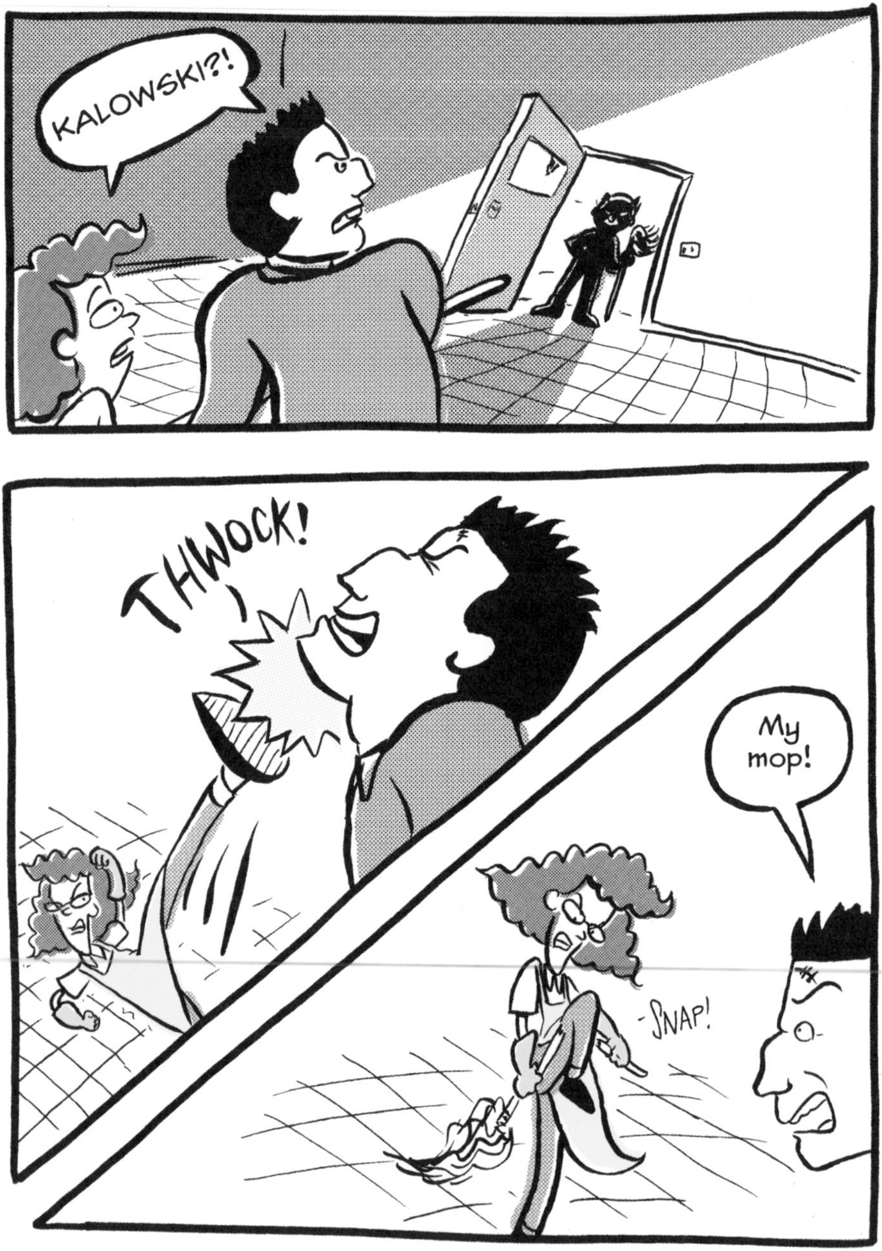
KALOWSKI?!
THWOCK!
My mop!
SNAP!

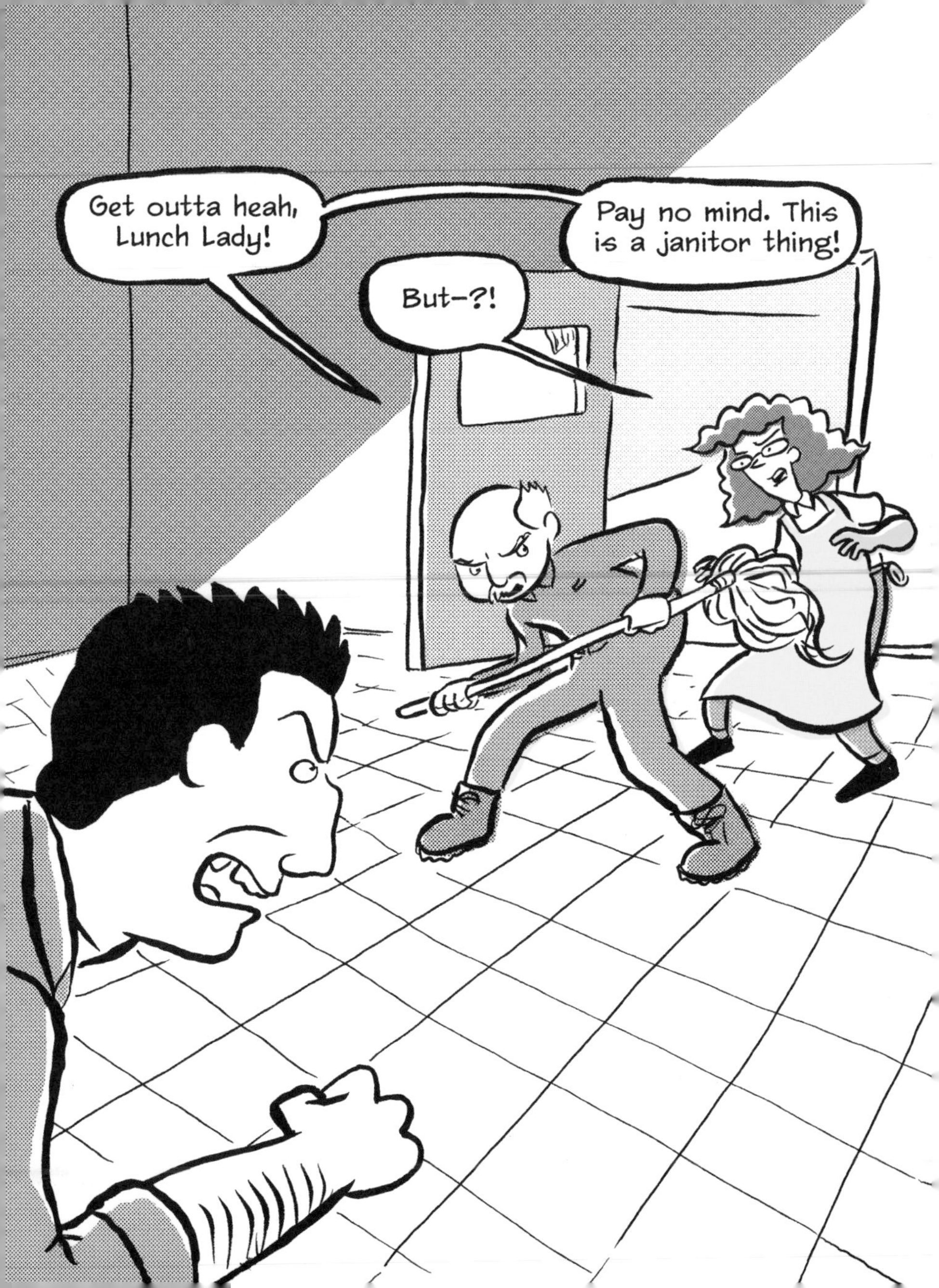
Get outta heah, Lunch Lady!
Pay no mind. This is a janitor thing!
But–?!

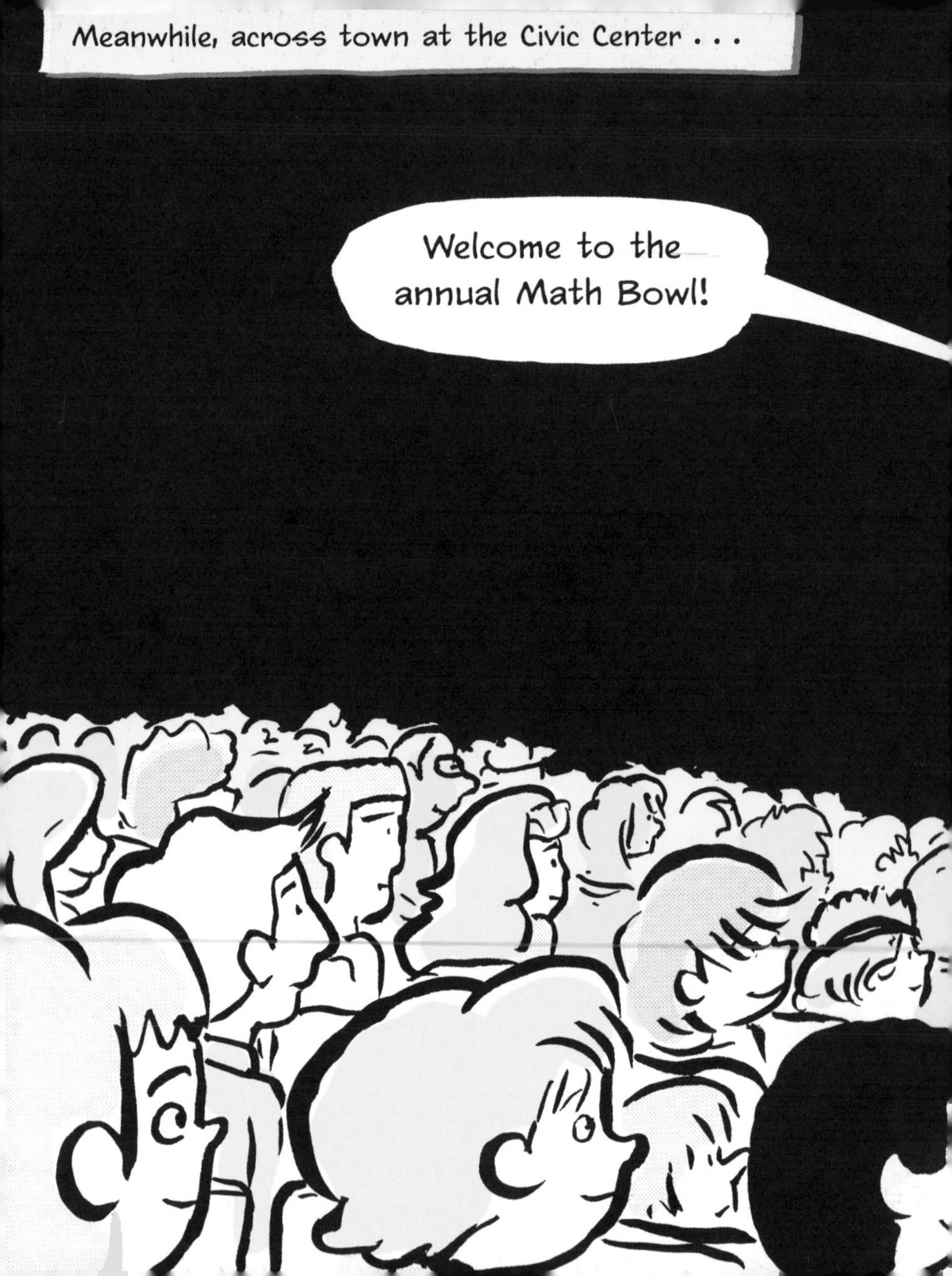
Meanwhile, across town at the Civic Center . . .
Welcome to the annual Math Bowl!

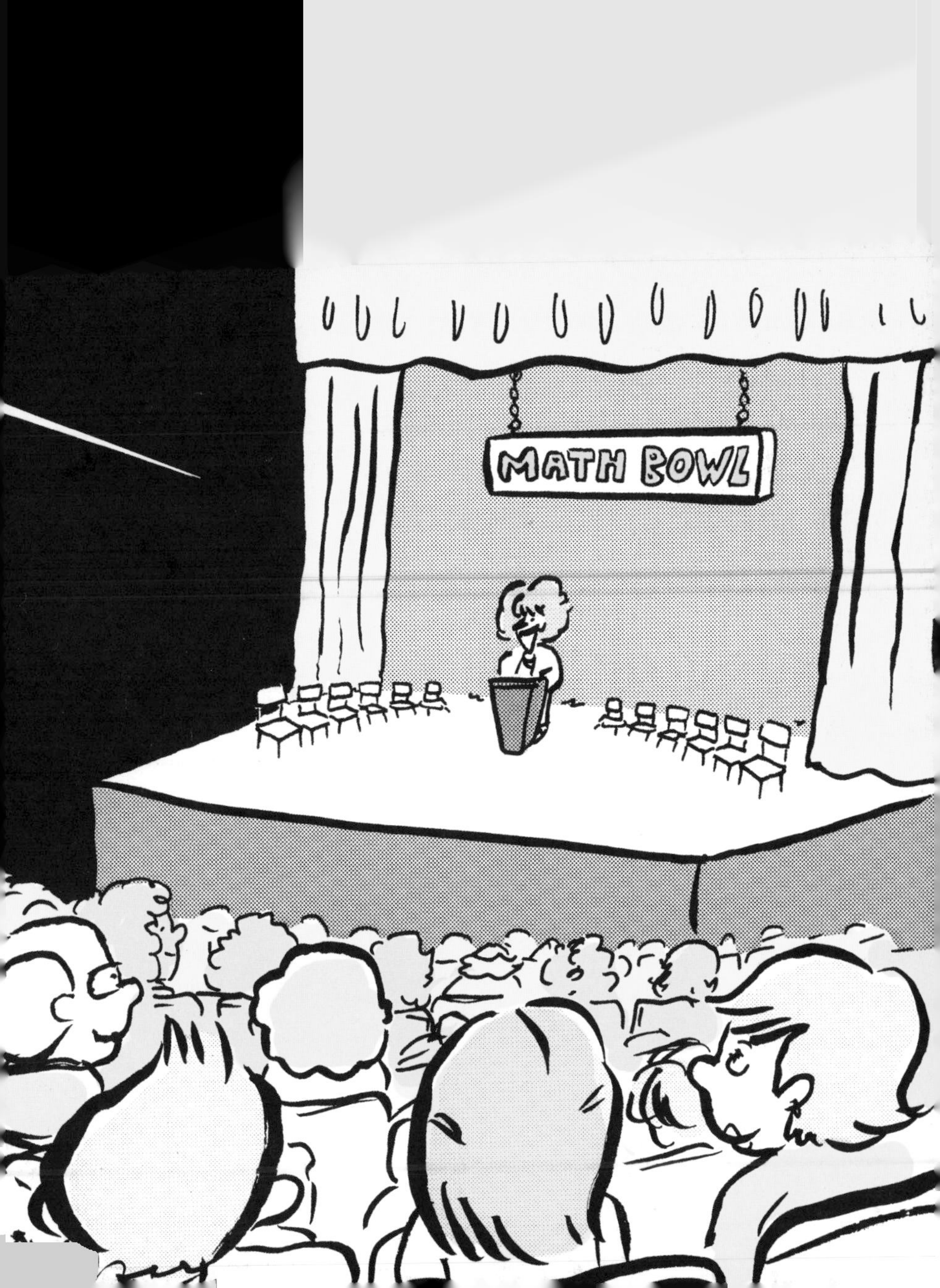
MATH BOWL

"Where the city's brightest go head to head in a math frenzy!"

"These students have fought hard all season long."

"And they're here tonight to win the title!"

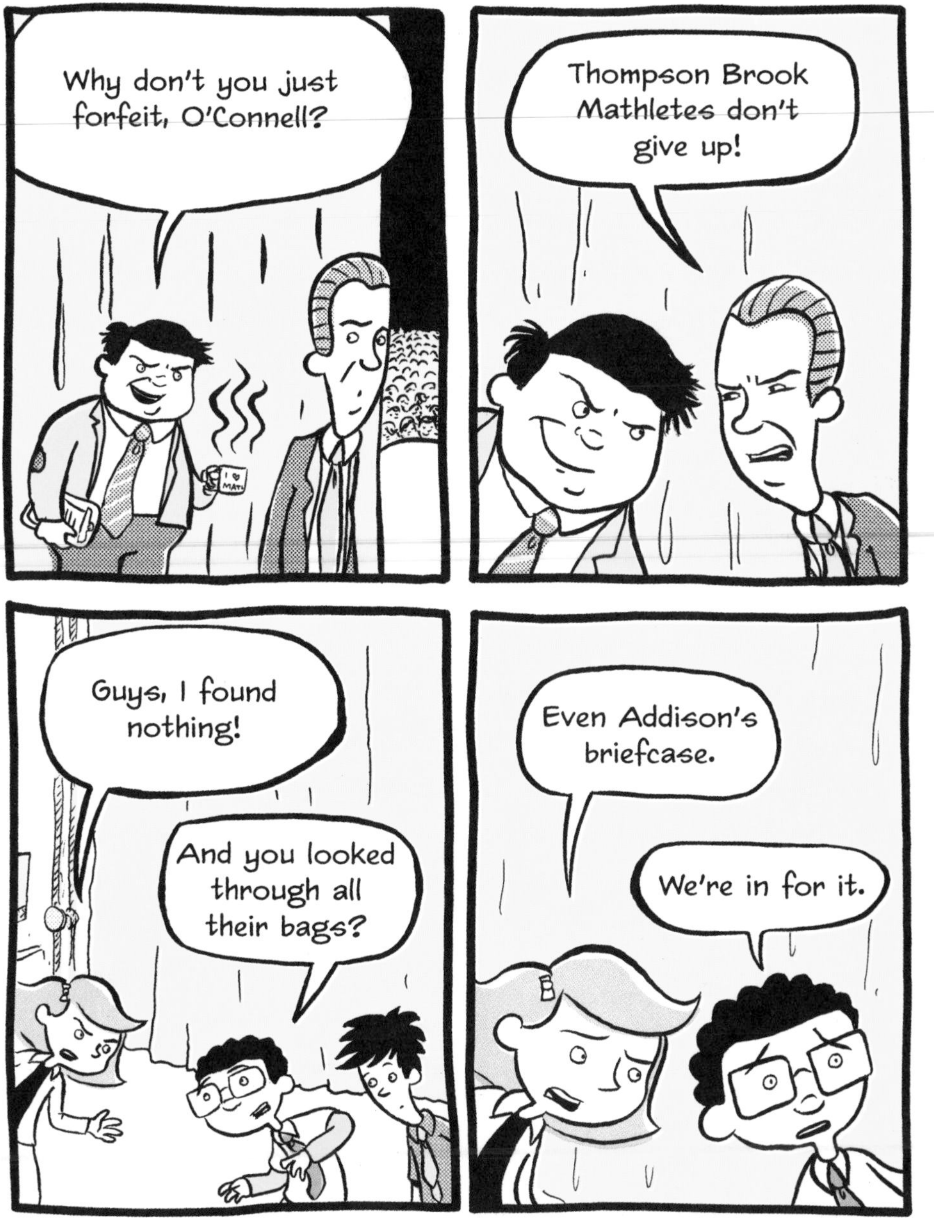
Why don't you just forfeit, O'Connell?
I ♡ MATH
Thompson Brook Mathletes don't give up!
Guys, I found nothing!
And you looked through all their bags?
Even Addison's briefcase.
We're in for it.

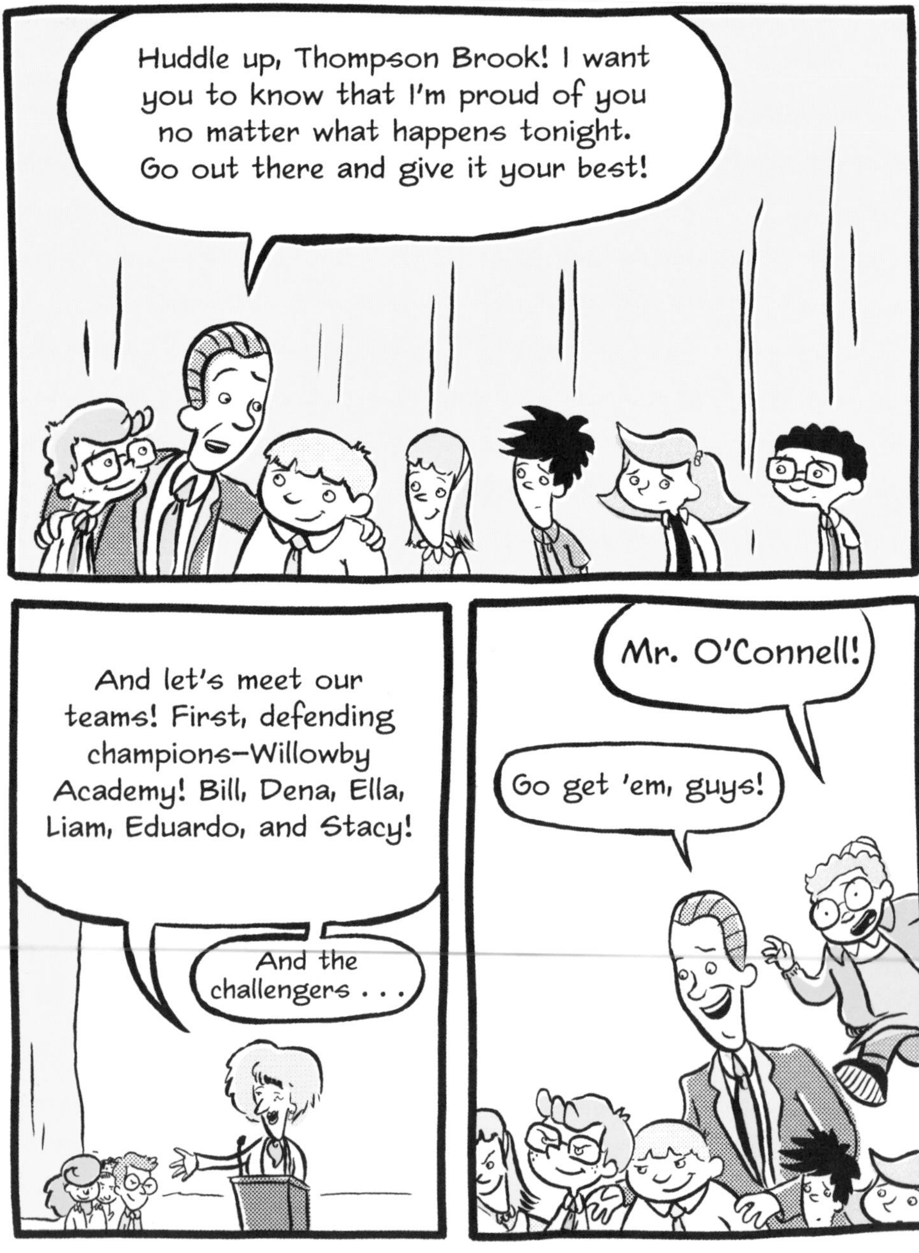
Huddle up, Thompson Brook! I want you to know that I'm proud of you no matter what happens tonight. Go out there and give it your best!
And let's meet our teams! First, defending champions—Willowby Academy! Bill, Dena, Ella, Liam, Eduardo, and Stacy!
And the challengers . . .
Mr. O'Connell!
Go get 'em, guys!

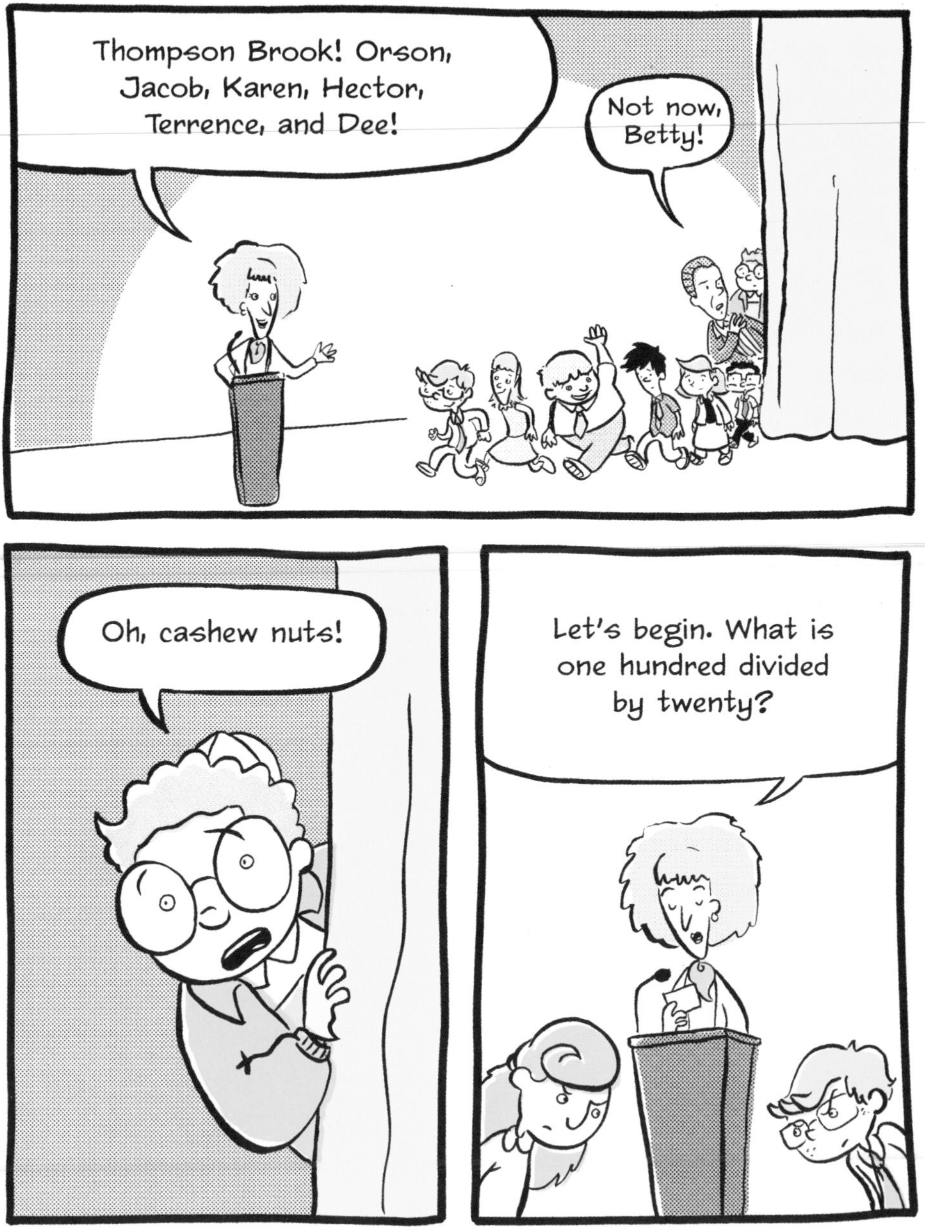
Thompson Brook! Orson, Jacob, Karen, Hector, Terrence, and Dee!
Not now, Betty!
Oh, cashew nuts!
Let's begin. What is one hundred divided by twenty?

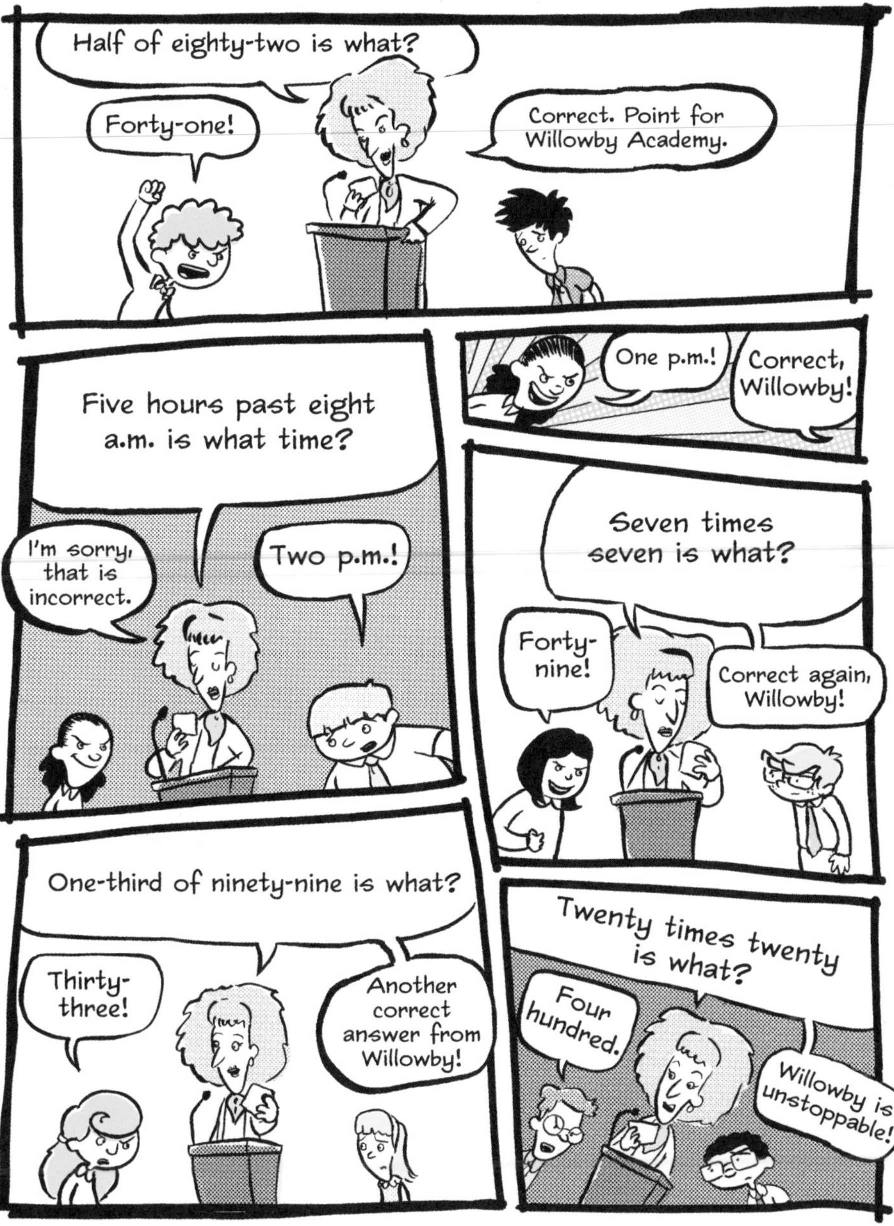

Half of eighty-two is what?
Forty-one!
Correct. Point for Willowby Academy.
Five hours past eight a.m. is what time?
Two p.m.!
I'm sorry, that is incorrect.
One p.m.!
Correct, Willowby!
Seven times seven is what?
Forty-nine!
Correct again, Willowby!
One-third of ninety-nine is what?
Thirty-three!
Another correct answer from Willowby!
Twenty times twenty is what?
Four hundred.
Willowby is unstoppable!

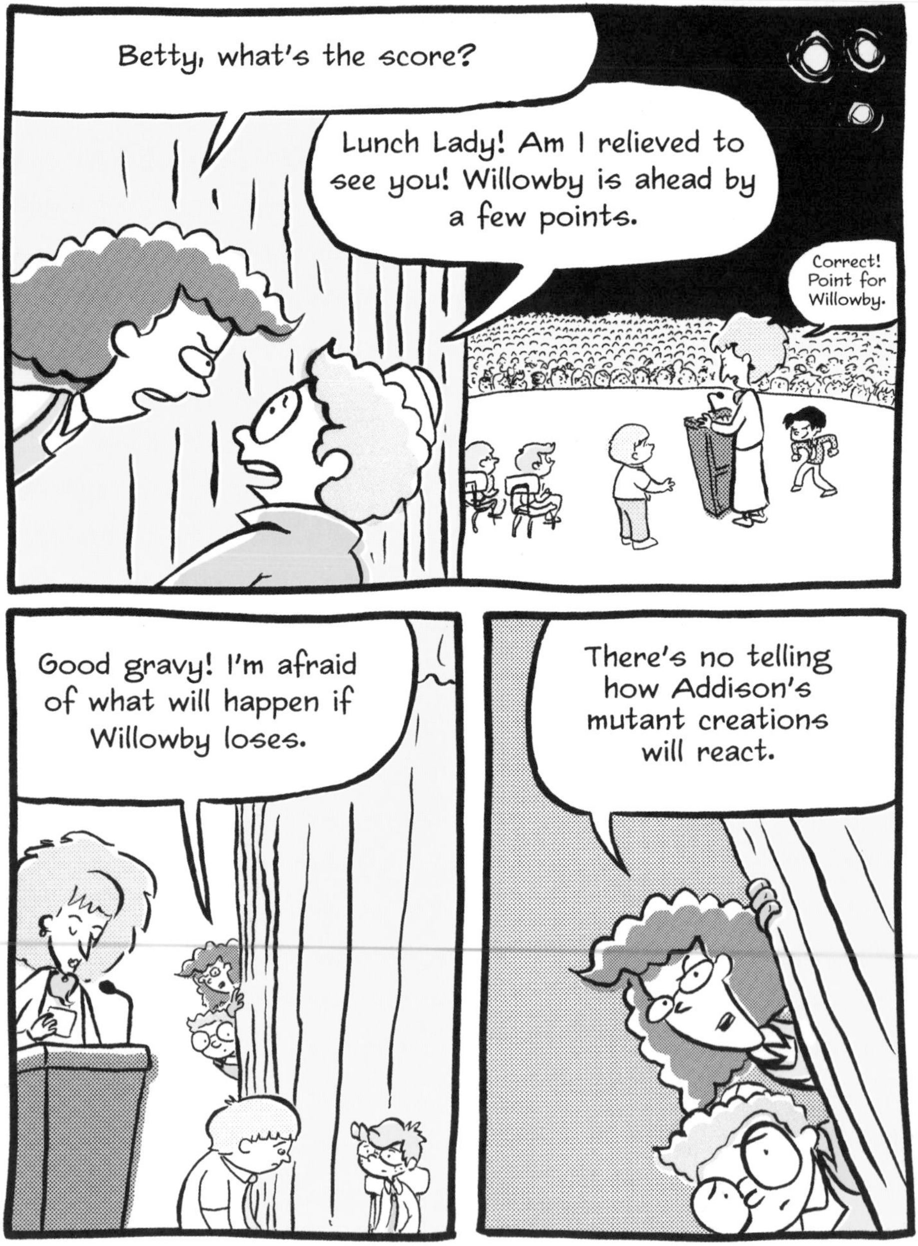
Betty, what's the score?
Lunch Lady! Am I relieved to see you! Willowby is ahead by a few points.
Correct! Point for Willowby.
Good gravy! I'm afraid of what will happen if Willowby loses.
There's no telling how Addison's mutant creations will react.

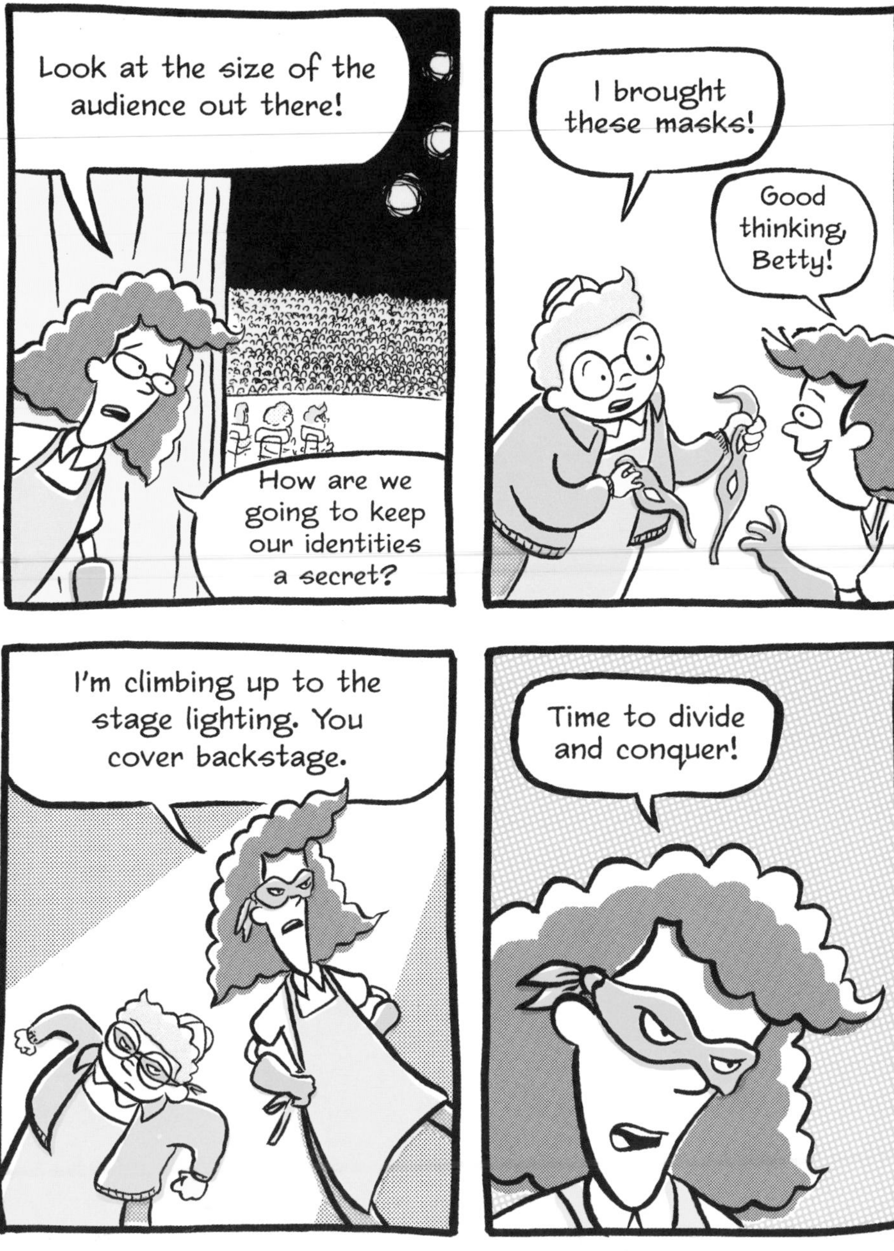
Look at the size of the audience out there!
How are we going to keep our identities a secret?
I brought these masks!
Good thinking, Betty!
I'm climbing up to the stage lighting. You cover backstage.
Time to divide and conquer!

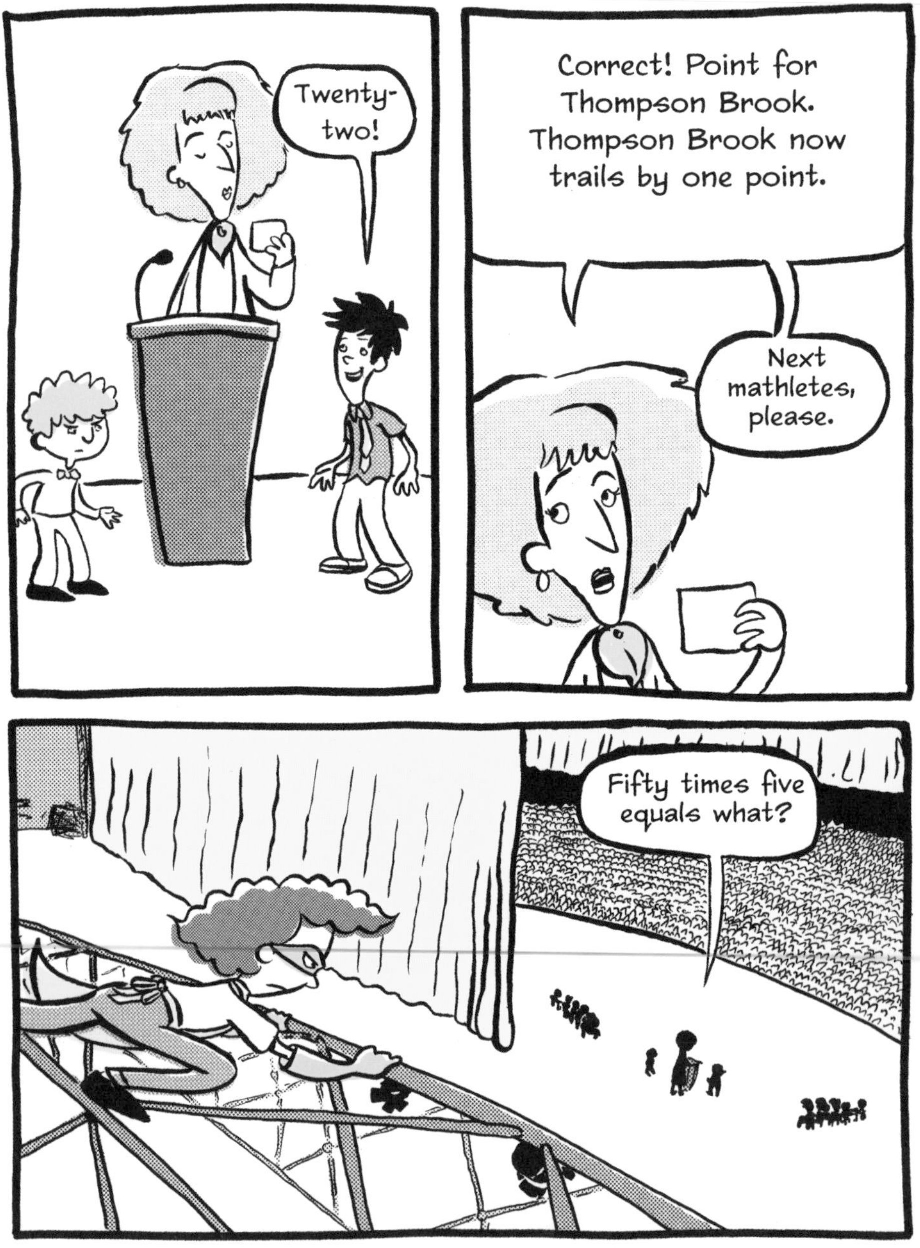
Twenty-two!
Correct! Point for Thompson Brook. Thompson Brook now trails by one point.
Next mathletes, please.
Fifty times five equals what?

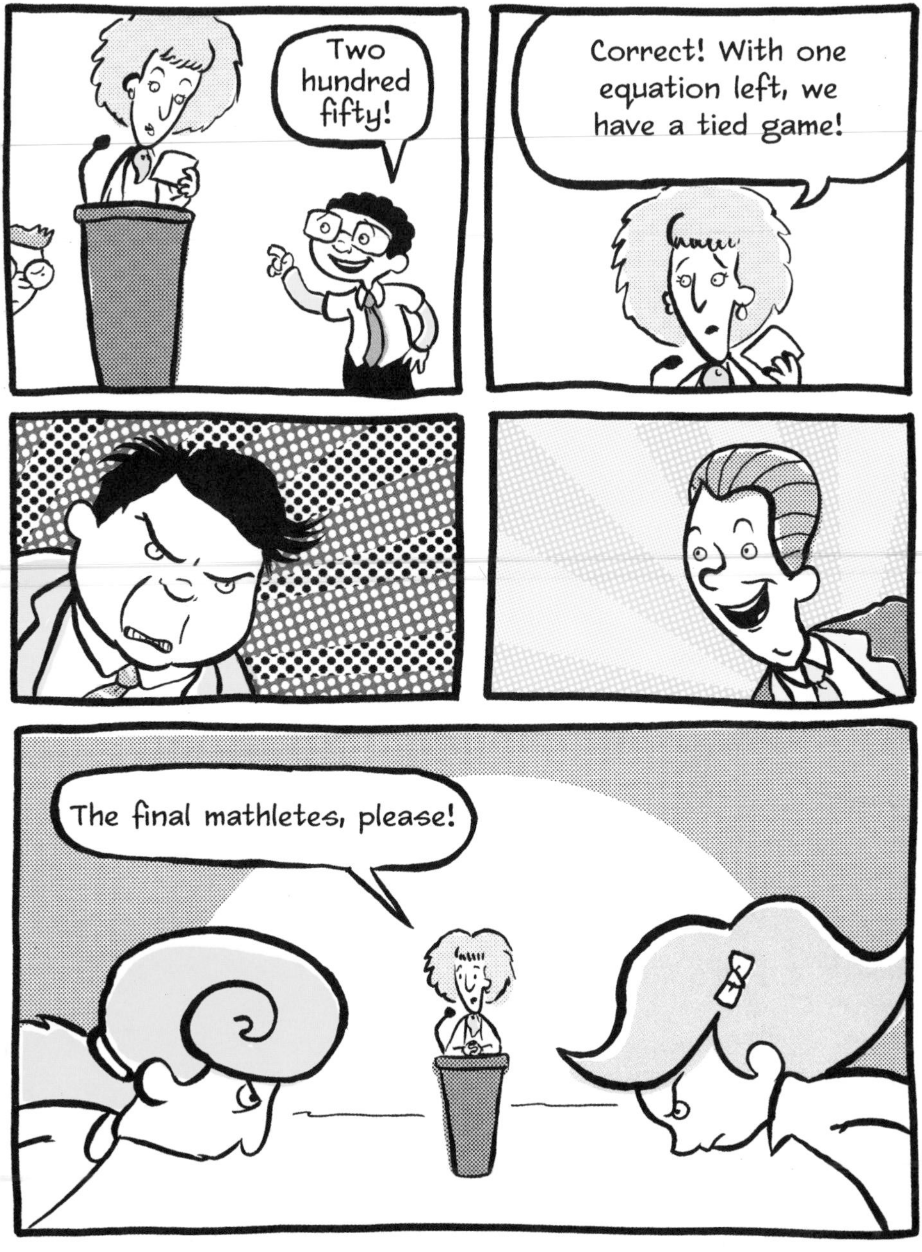
Two hundred fifty!
Correct! With one equation left, we have a tied game!
The final mathletes, please!

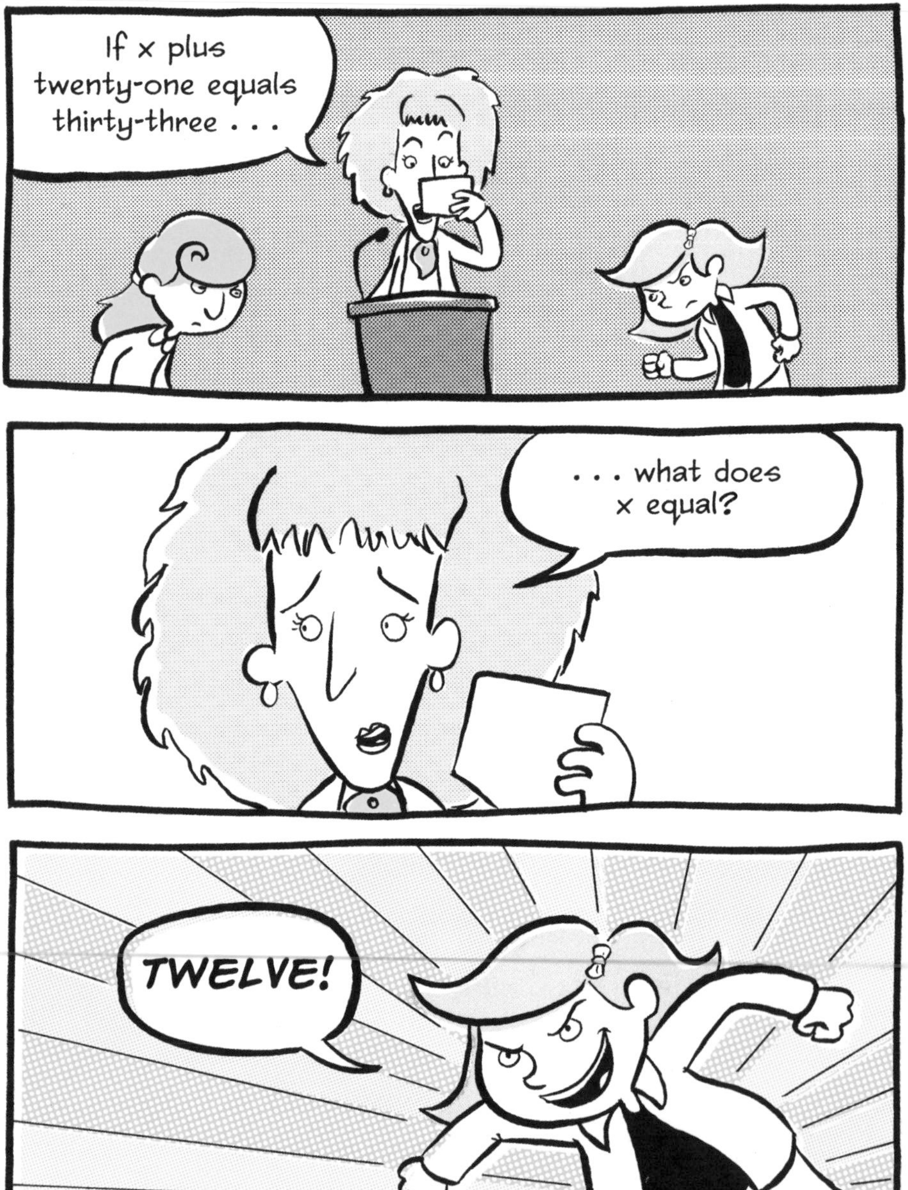
If x plus twenty-one equals thirty-three . . .
. . . what does x equal?
TWELVE!

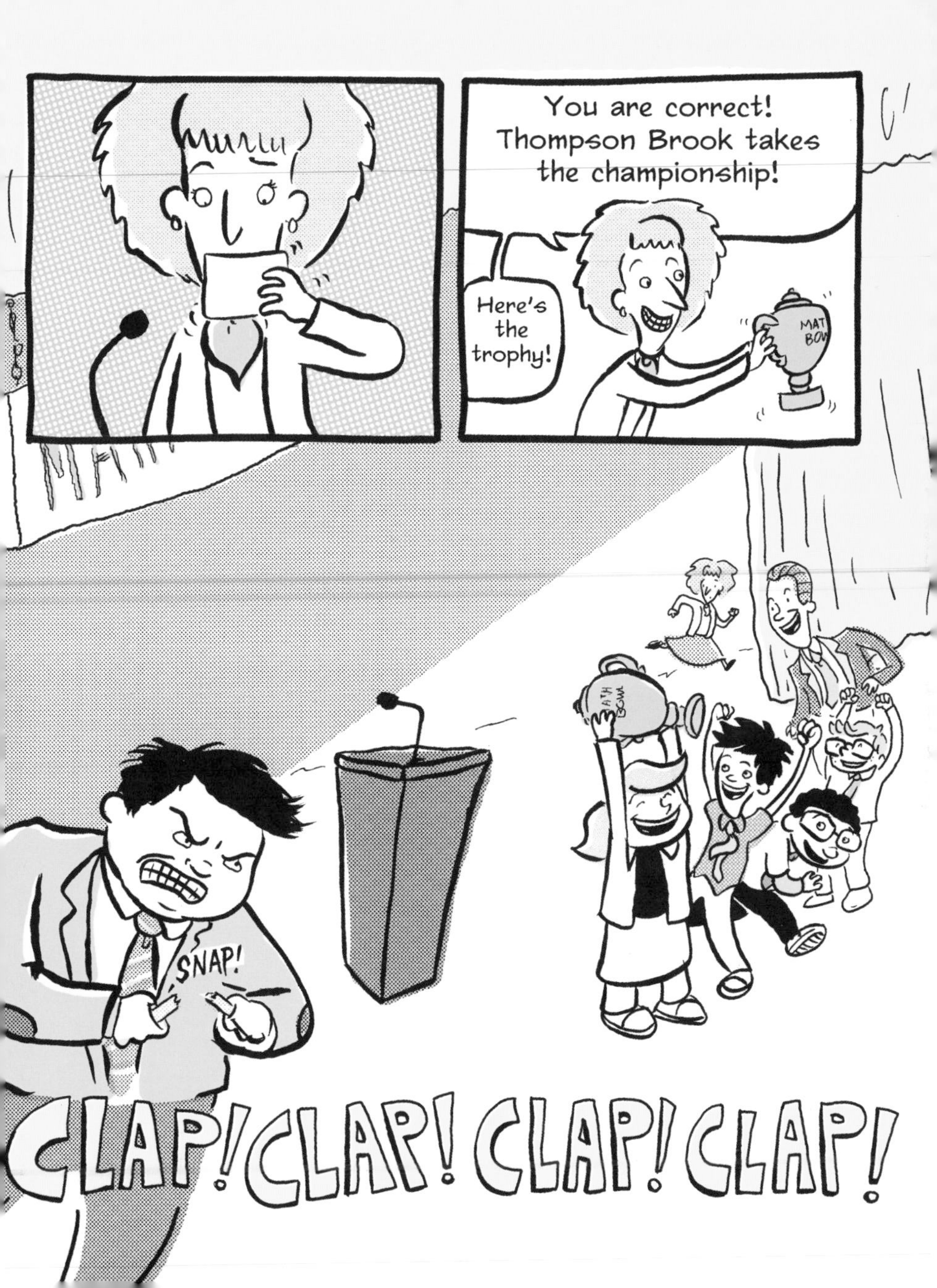
You are correct! Thompson Brook takes the championship!
Here's the trophy!
MATH BOWL
SNAP!
CLAP! CLAP! CLAP! CLAP!

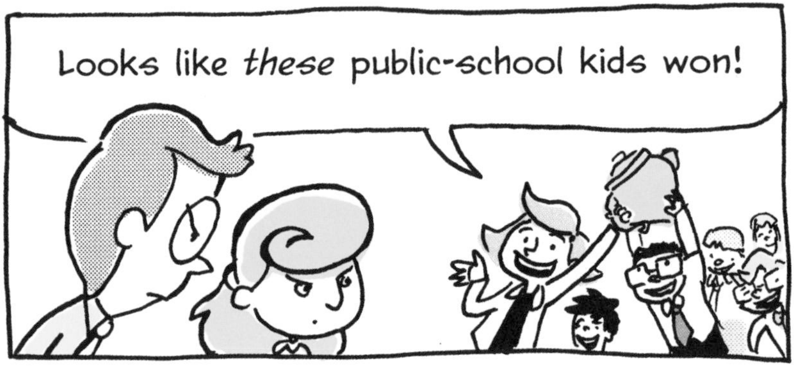
Looks like *these* public-school kids won!

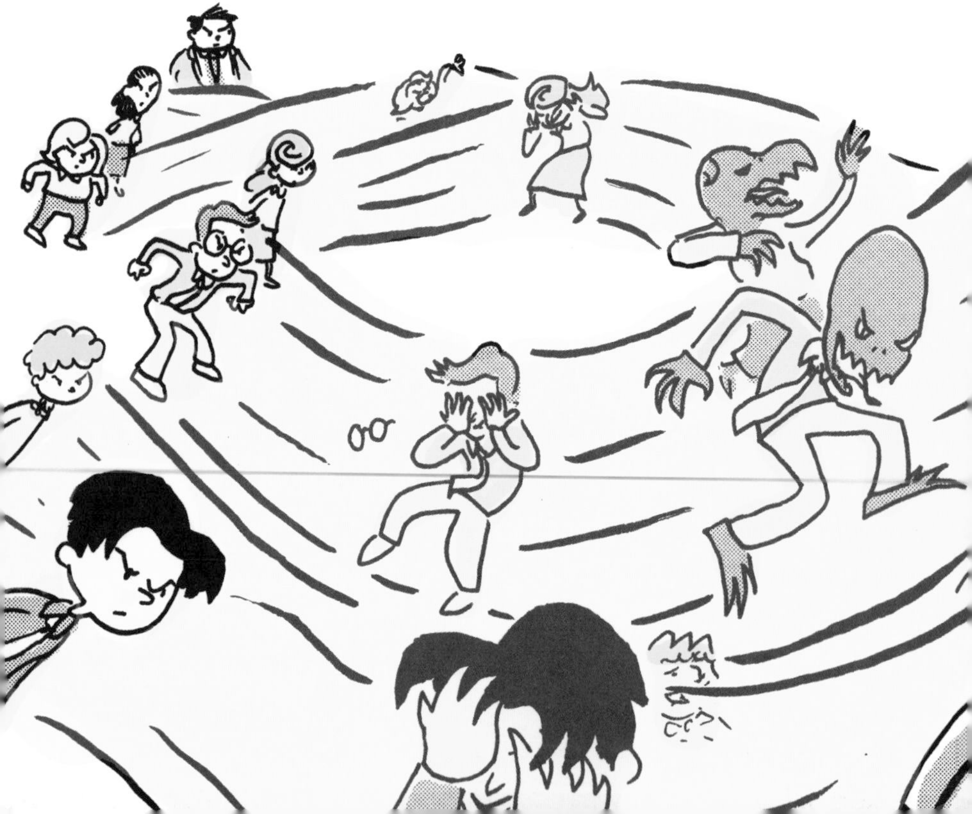

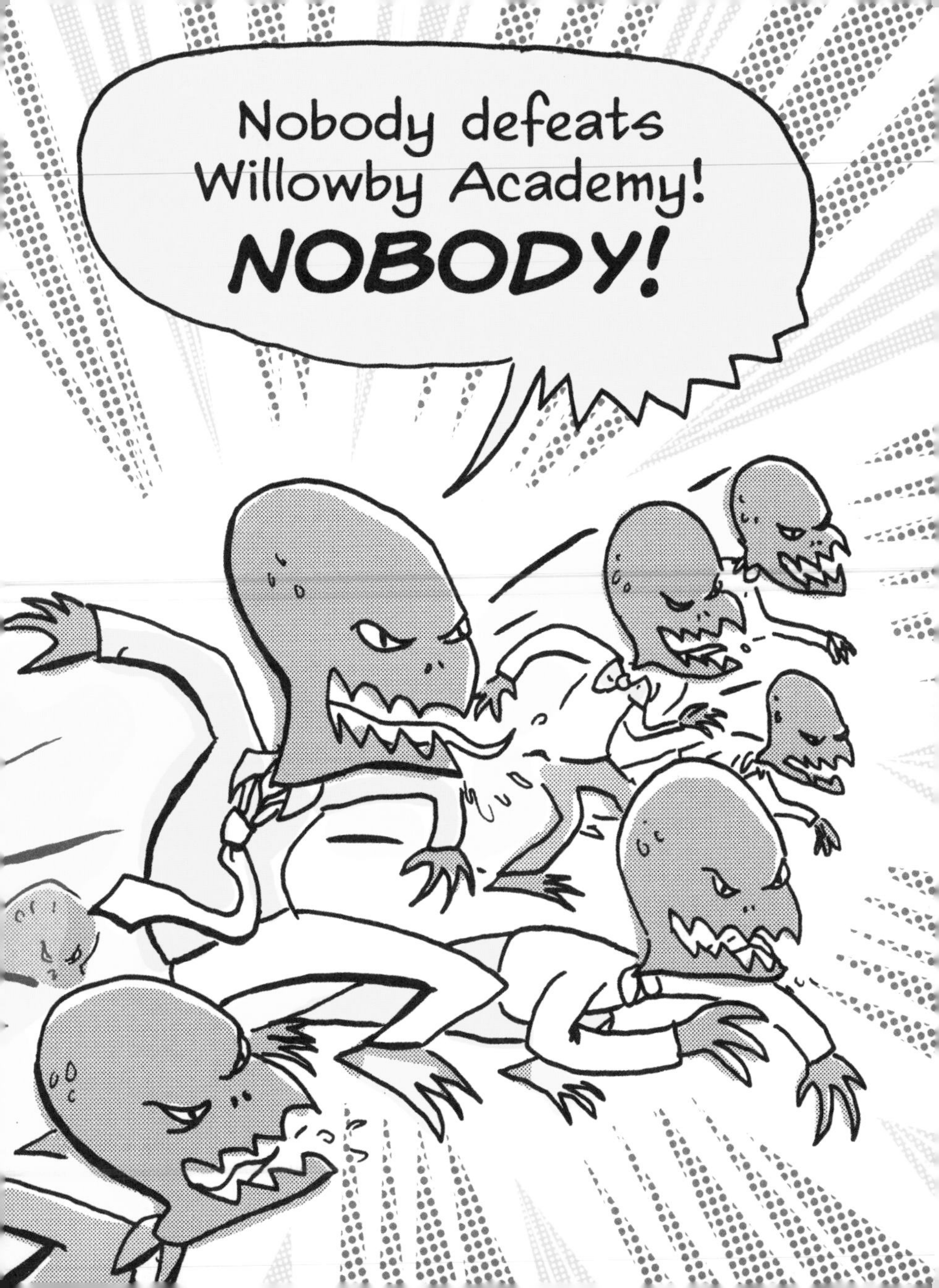
Nobody defeats Willowby Academy! NOBODY!

AGHHHHHHH
That trophy is ours!
Dee, j-j-just give them the trophy!
No way! It's ours!

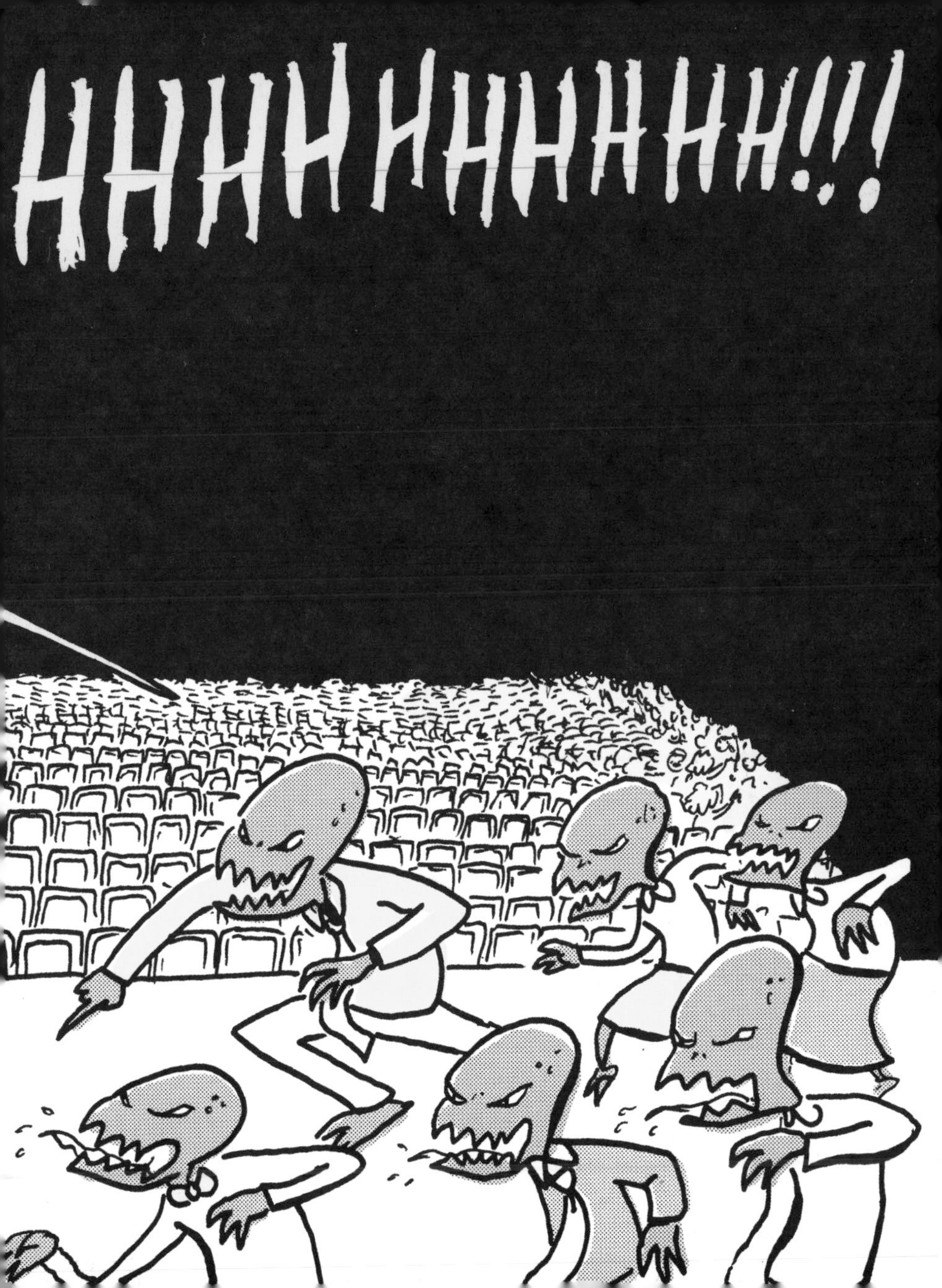
HHHHHHHHHHHH!!!

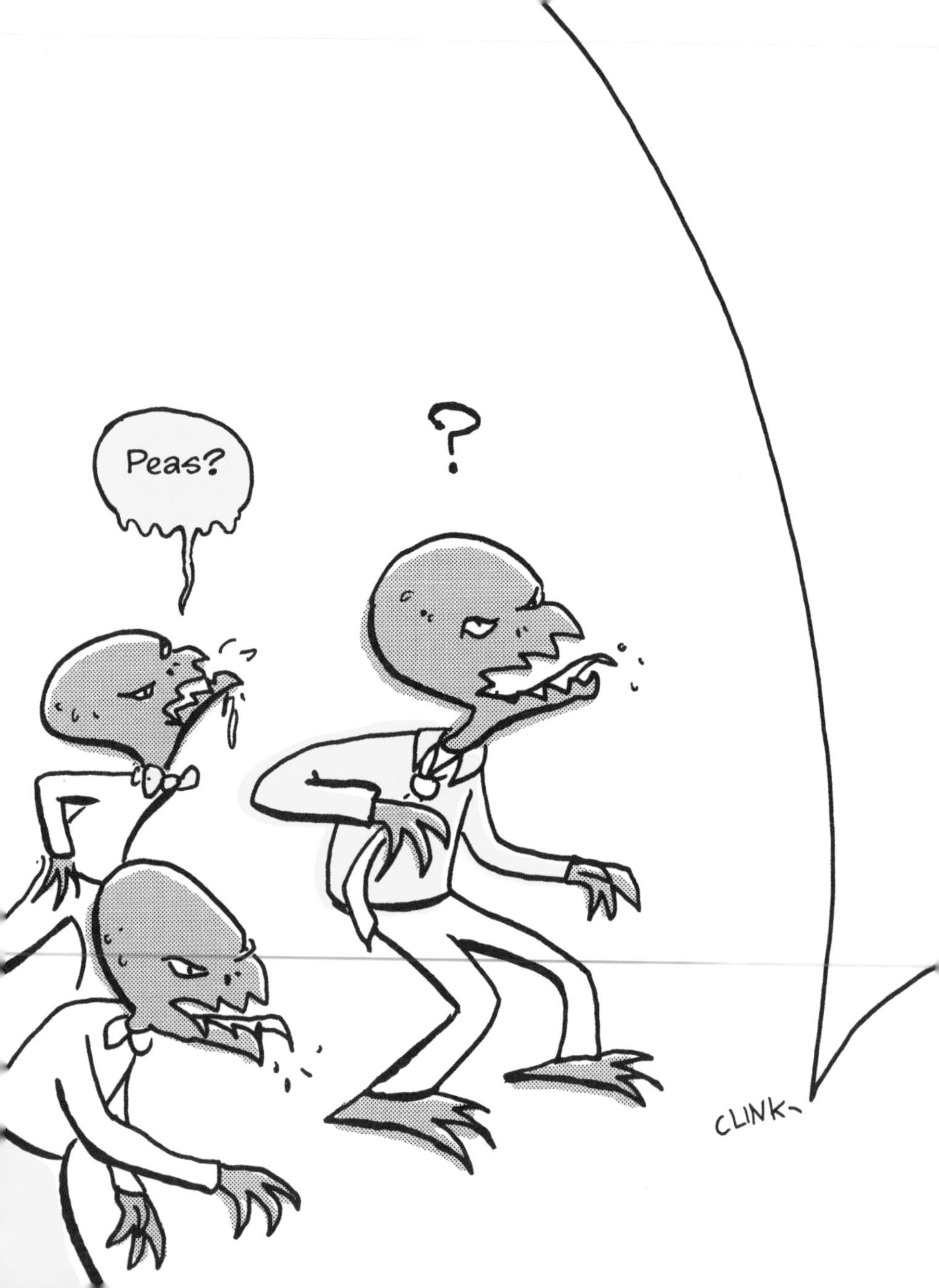
Peas?
?
CLINK-

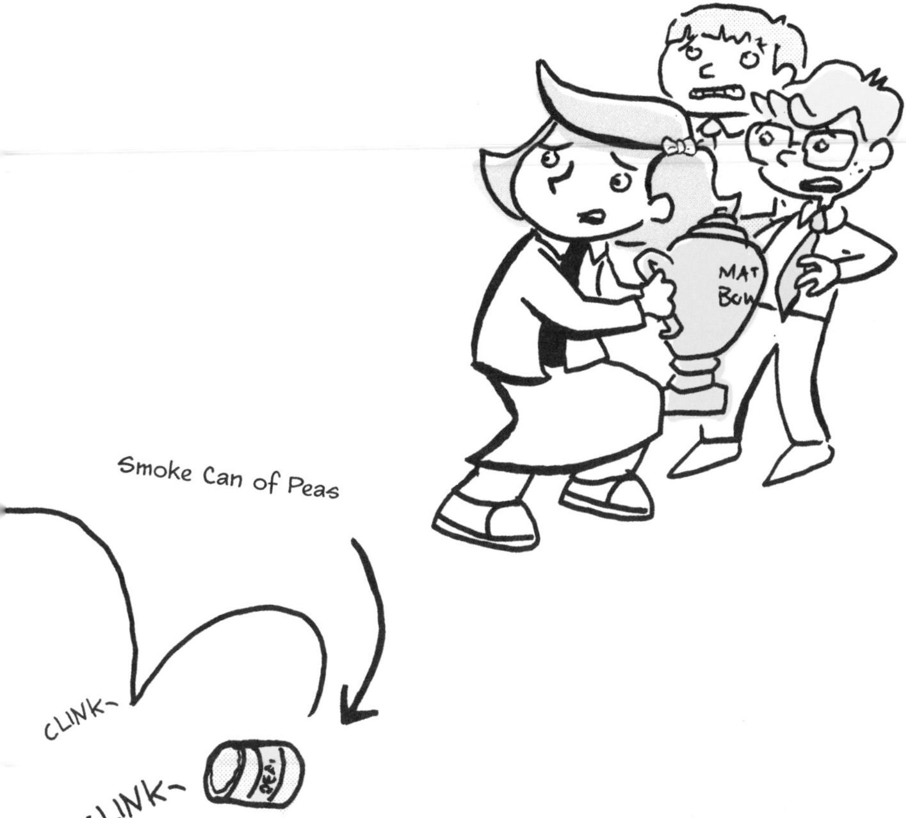
MAT
BOW
Smoke Can of Peas
CLINK-
CLINK-
PEAS

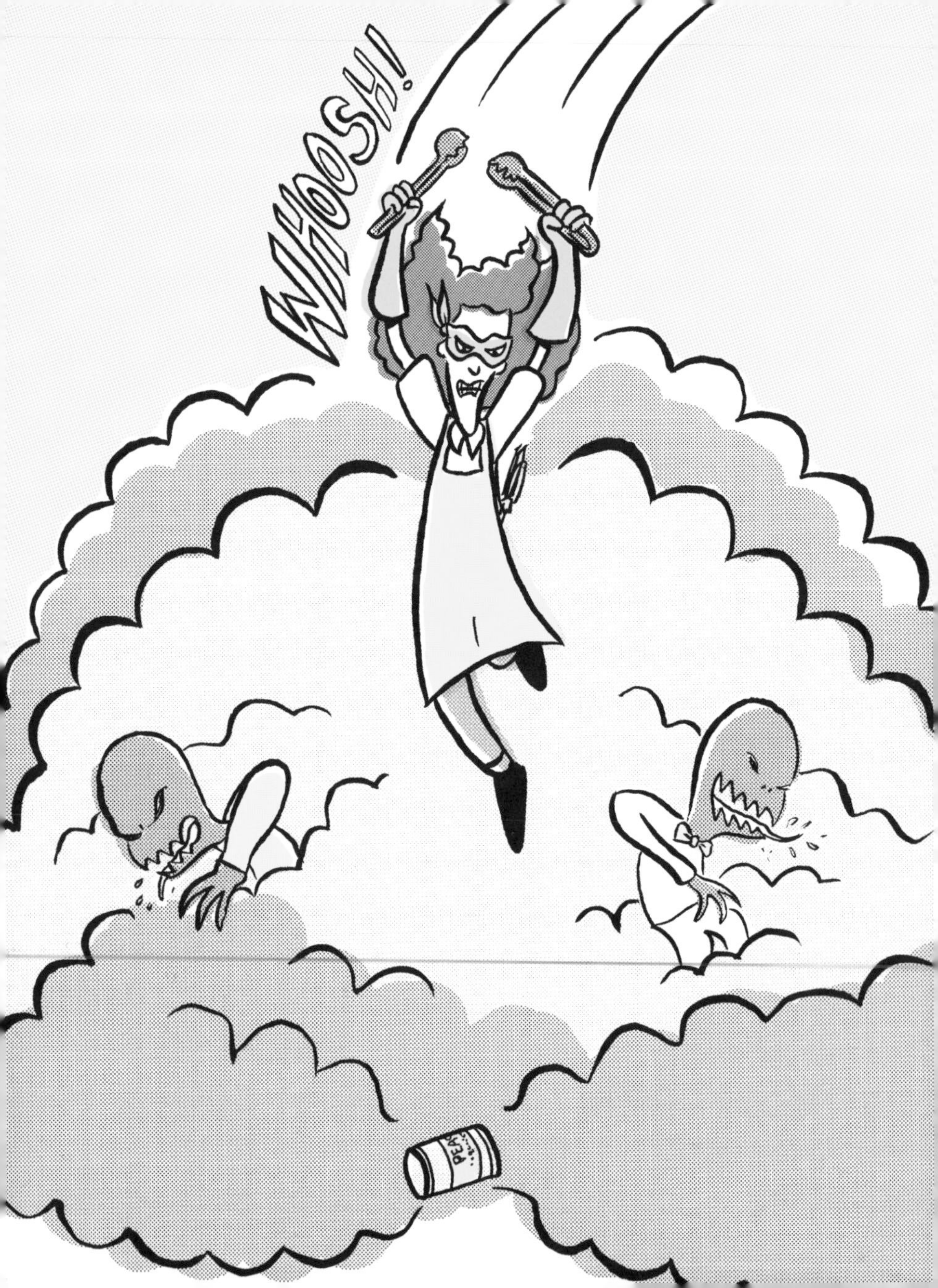
WHOOSH!
PEAS

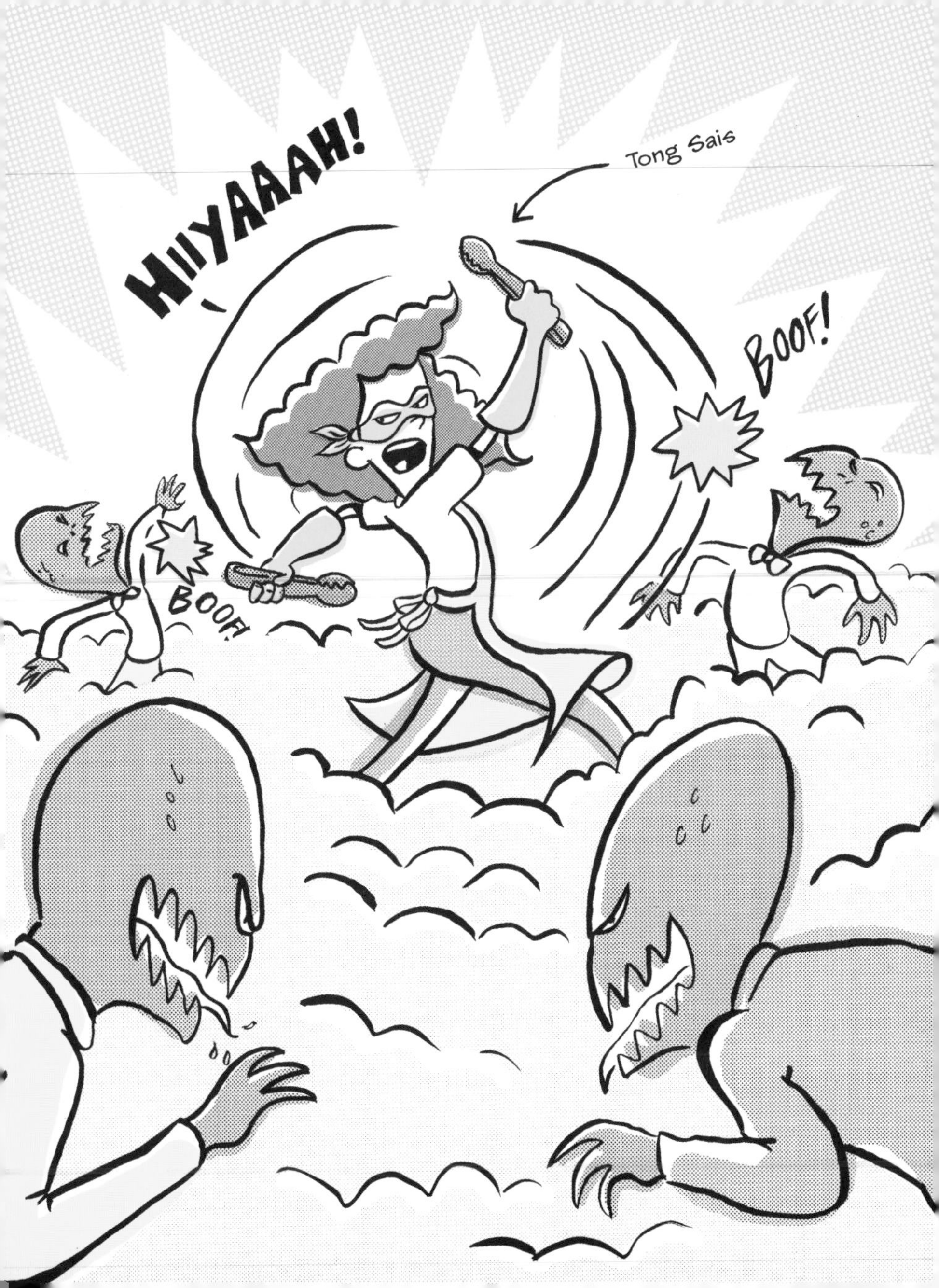
HIIYAAAH!
Tong Sais
BOOF!
BOOF!

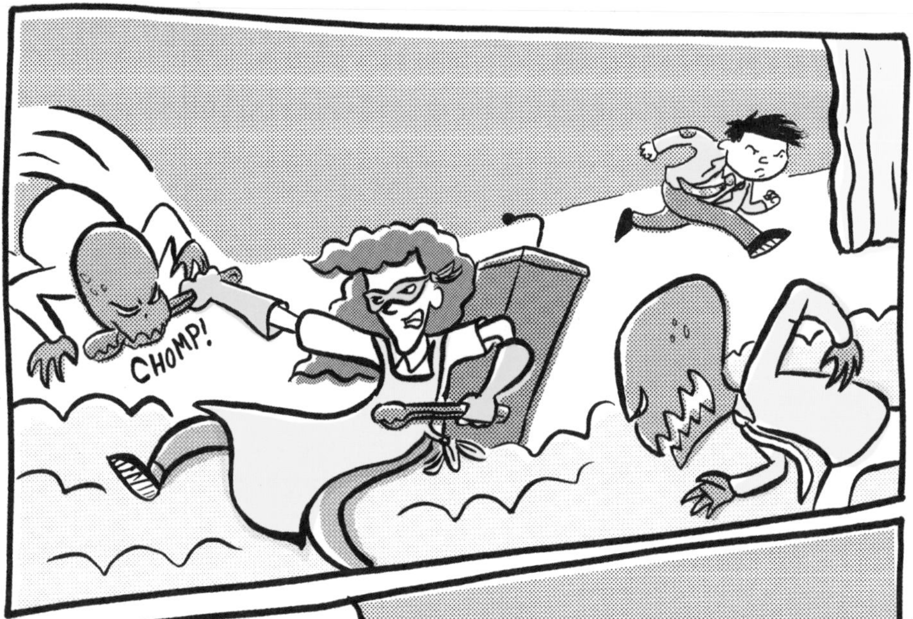
CHOMP!

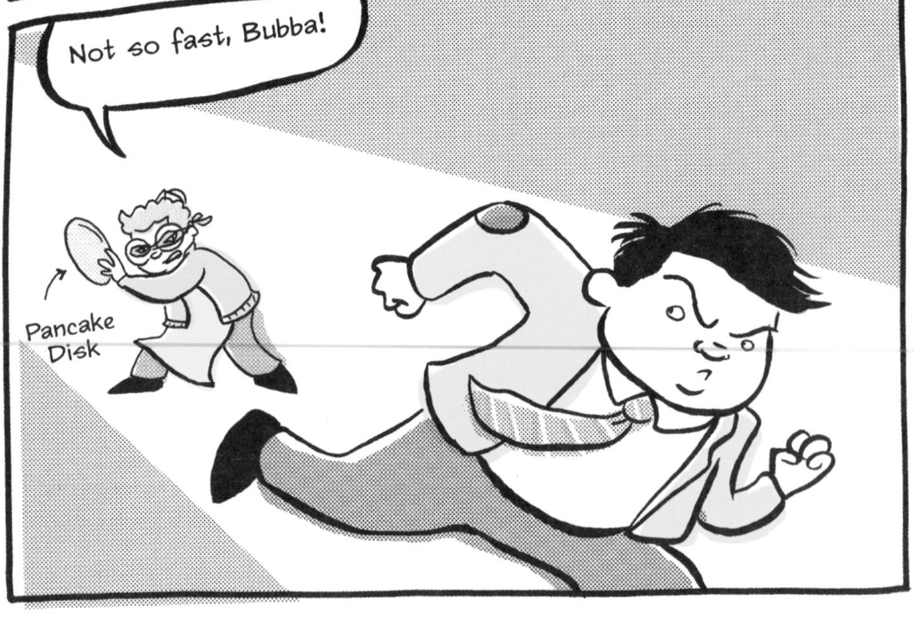
Not so fast, Bubba!
Pancake Disk

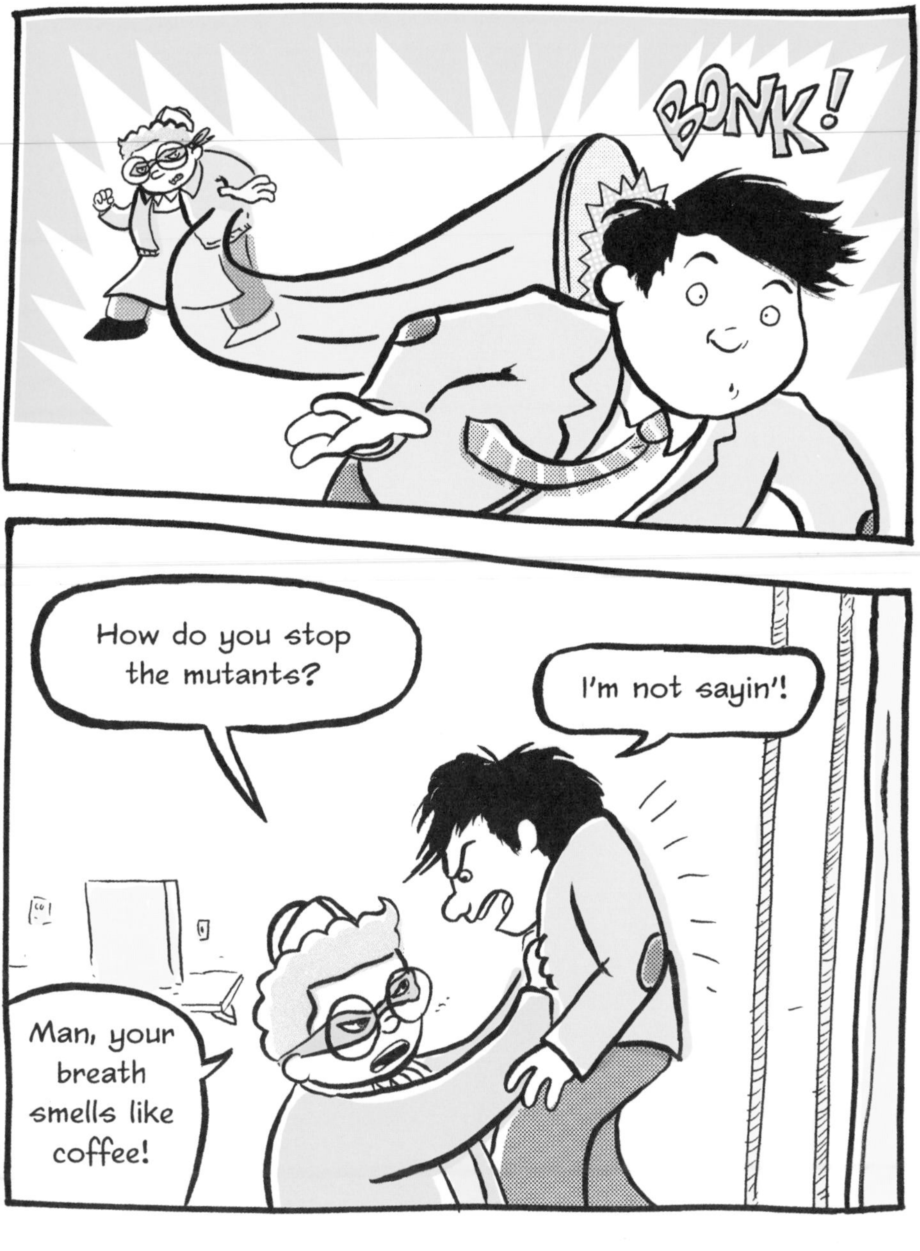
BONK!
How do you stop the mutants?
I'm not sayin'!
Man, your breath smells like coffee!

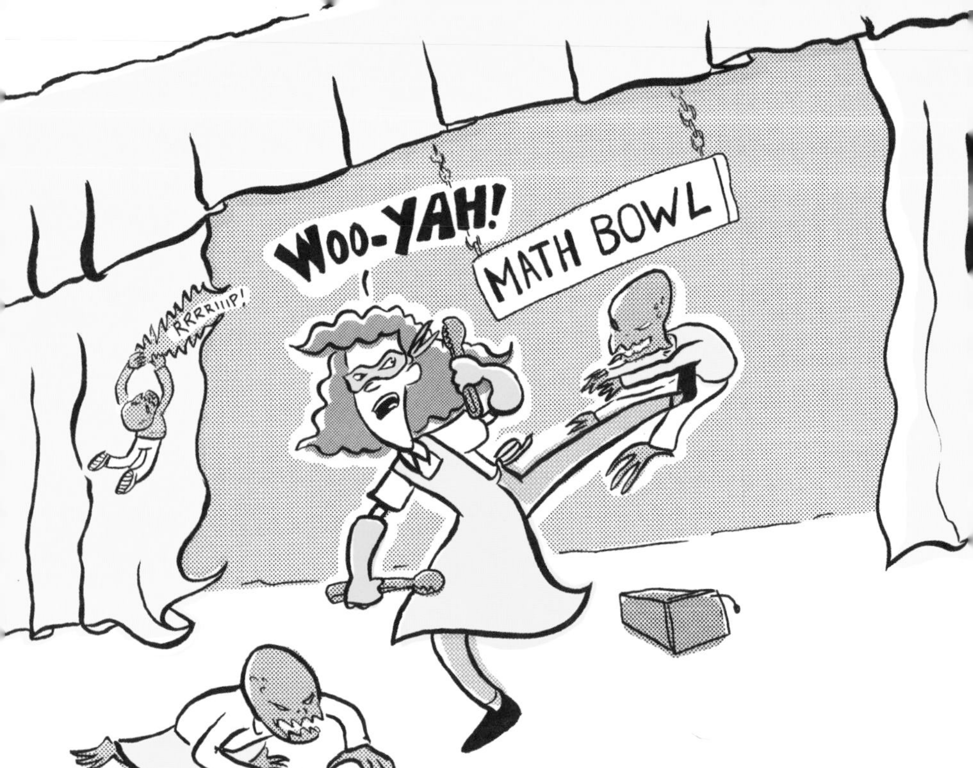
RRRRIIIP!
WOO-YAH!
MATH BOWL

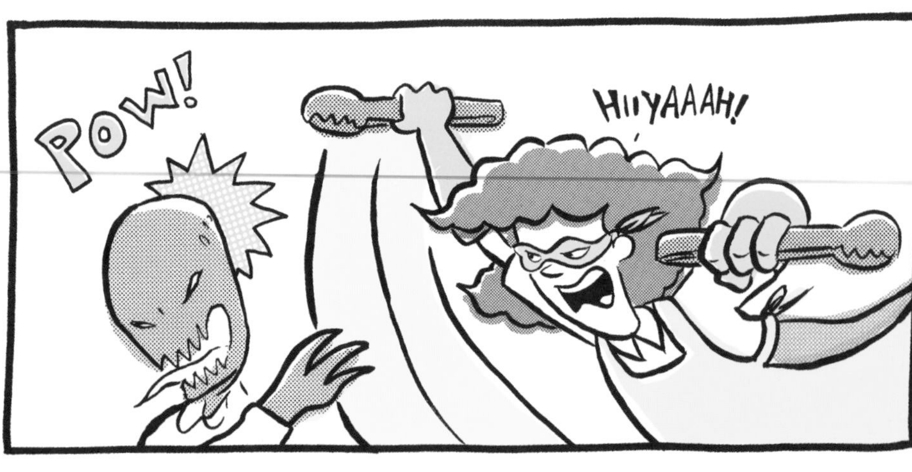
POW!
HIIYAAAH!

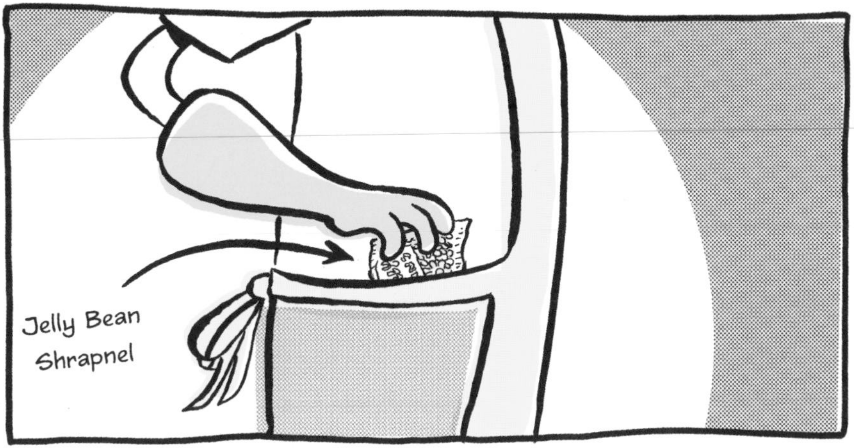
Jelly Bean Shrapnel

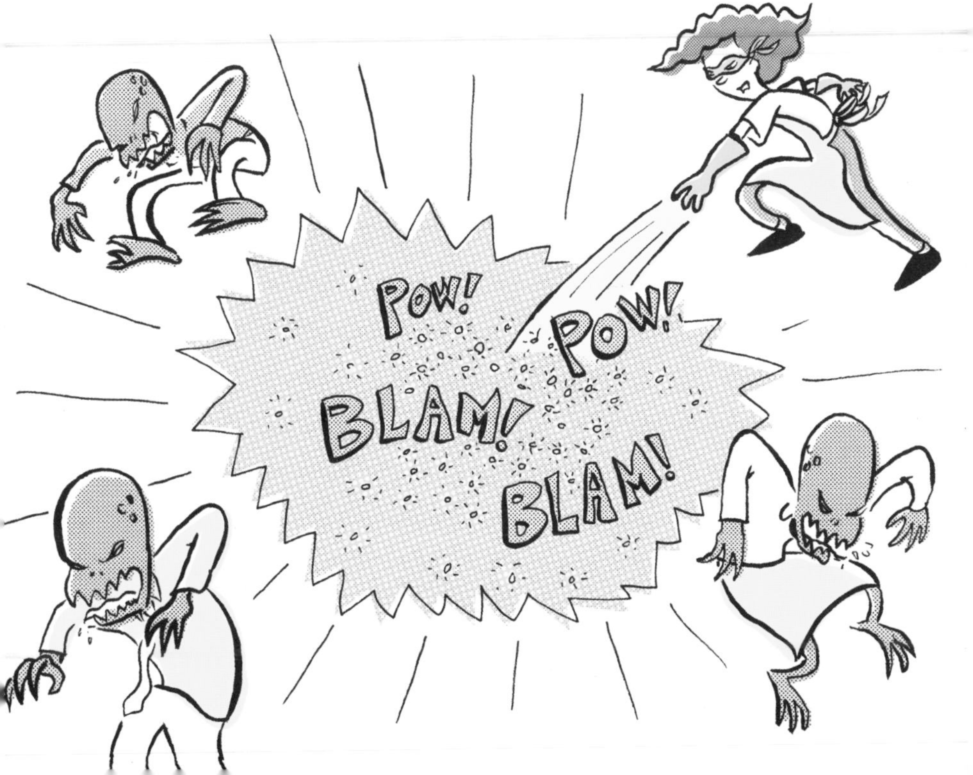
POW!
POW!
BLAM!
BLAM!

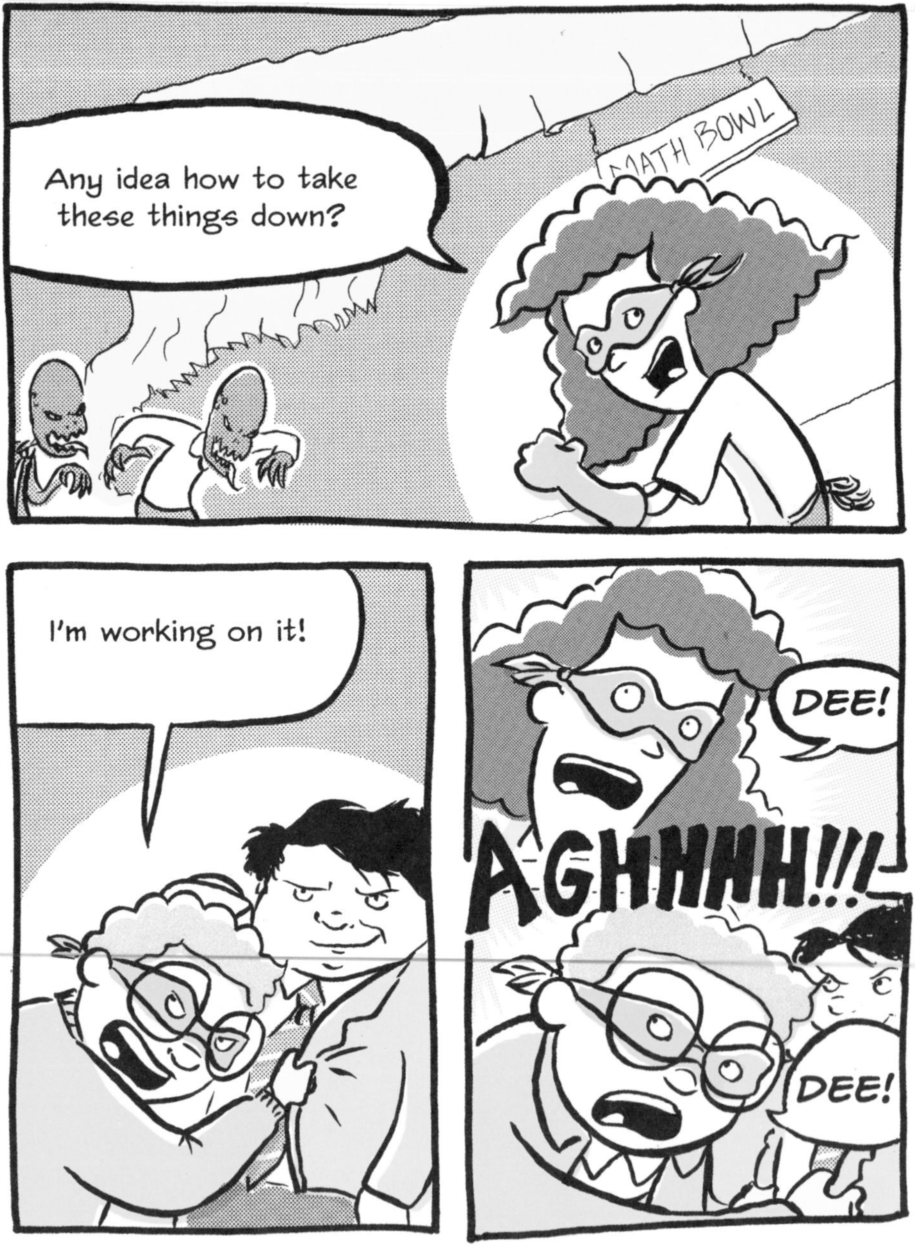
MATH BOWL
Any idea how to take these things down?
I'm working on it!
DEE!
AGHHHH!!!
DEE!

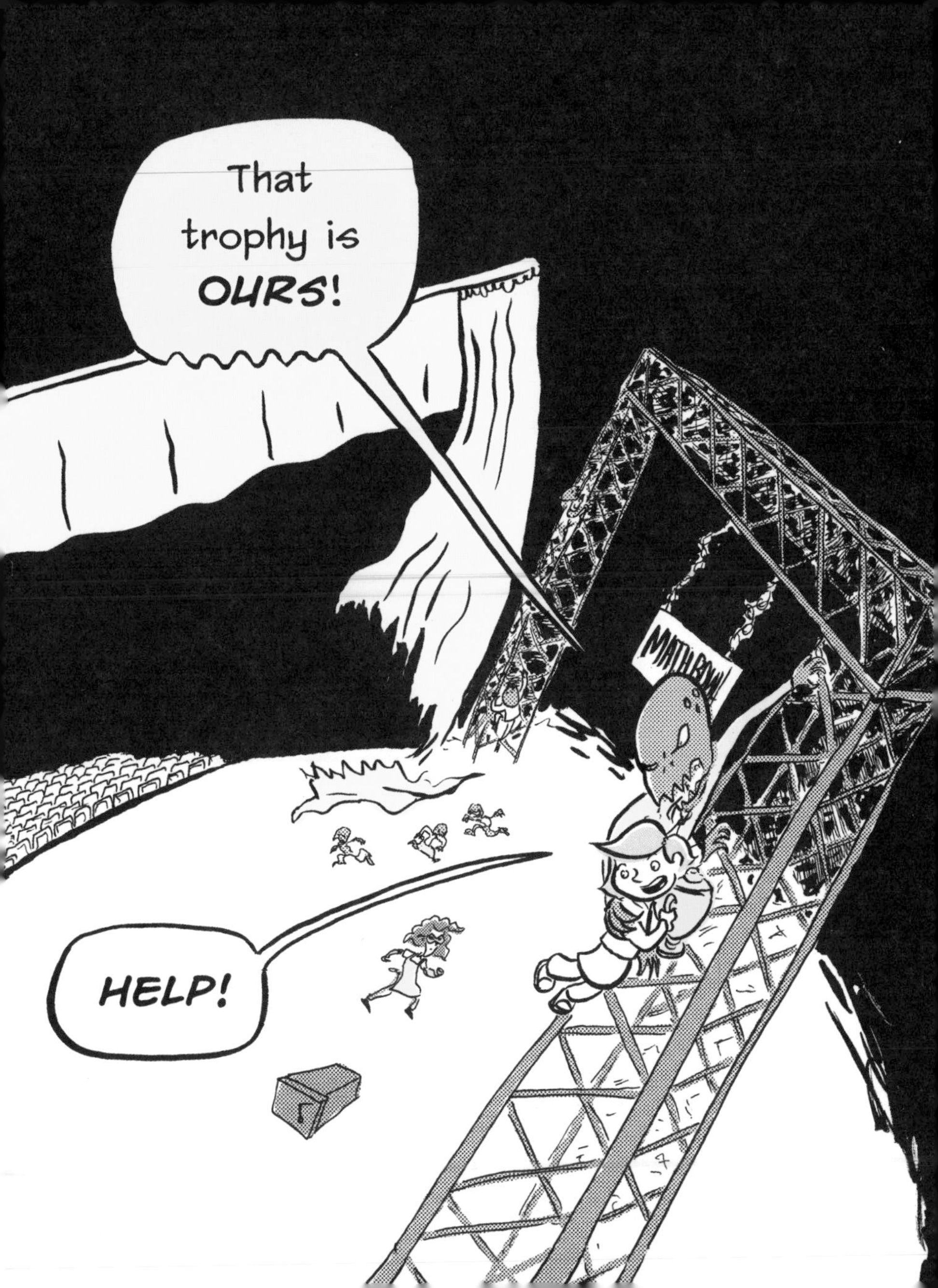
That trophy is OURS!
MATH BOWL
HELP!

Mustard Grappling Hook

'clink!

POOF!

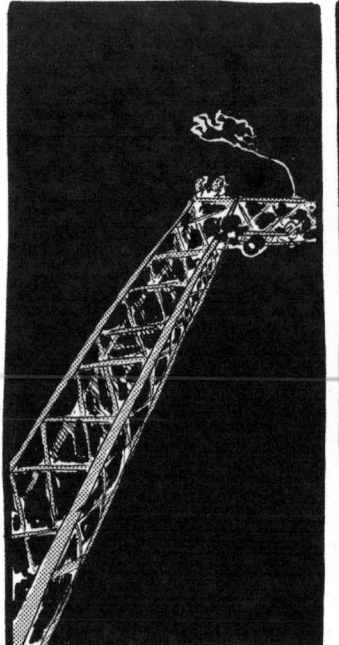

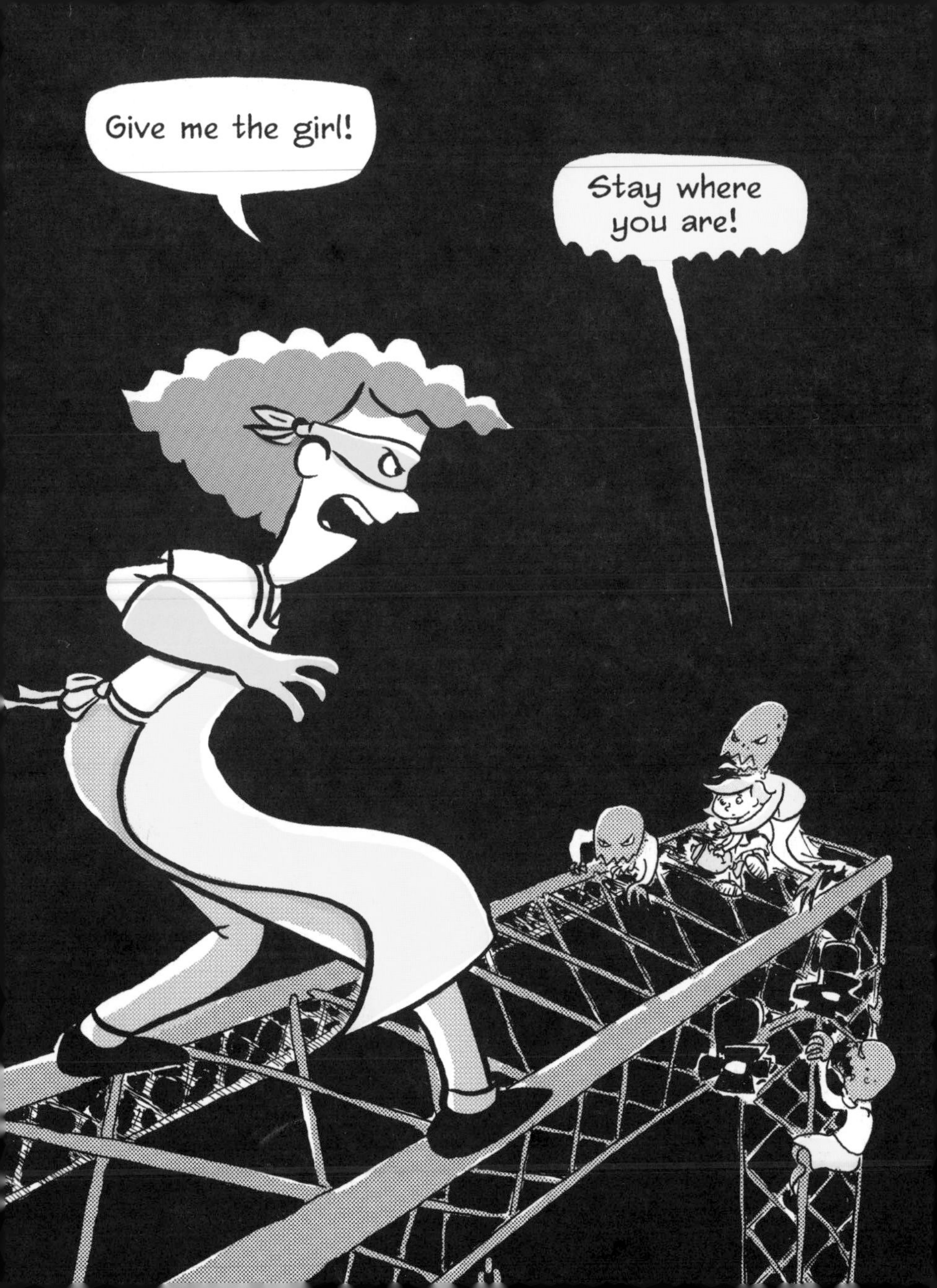
Give me the girl!
Stay where you are!

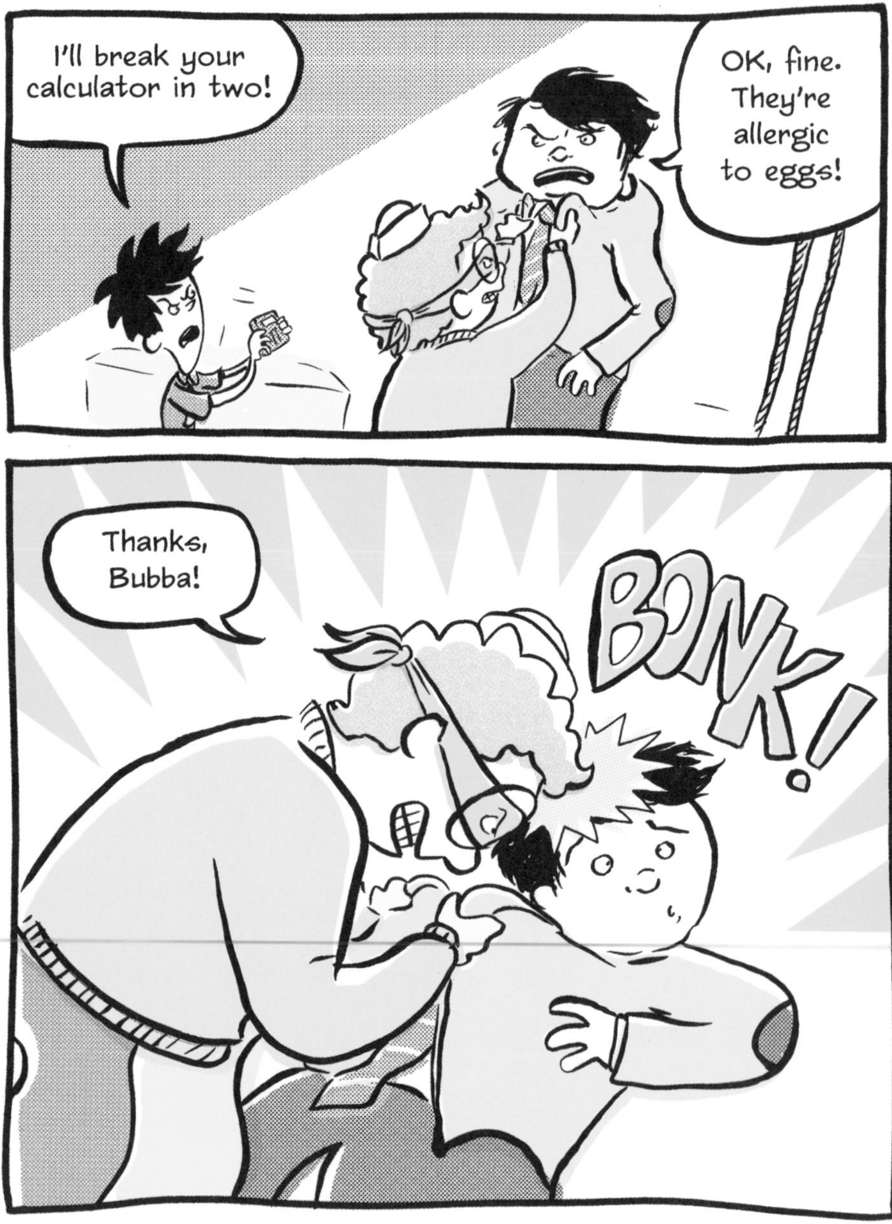
I'll break your calculator in two!
OK, fine. They're allergic to eggs!
Thanks, Bubba!
BONK!

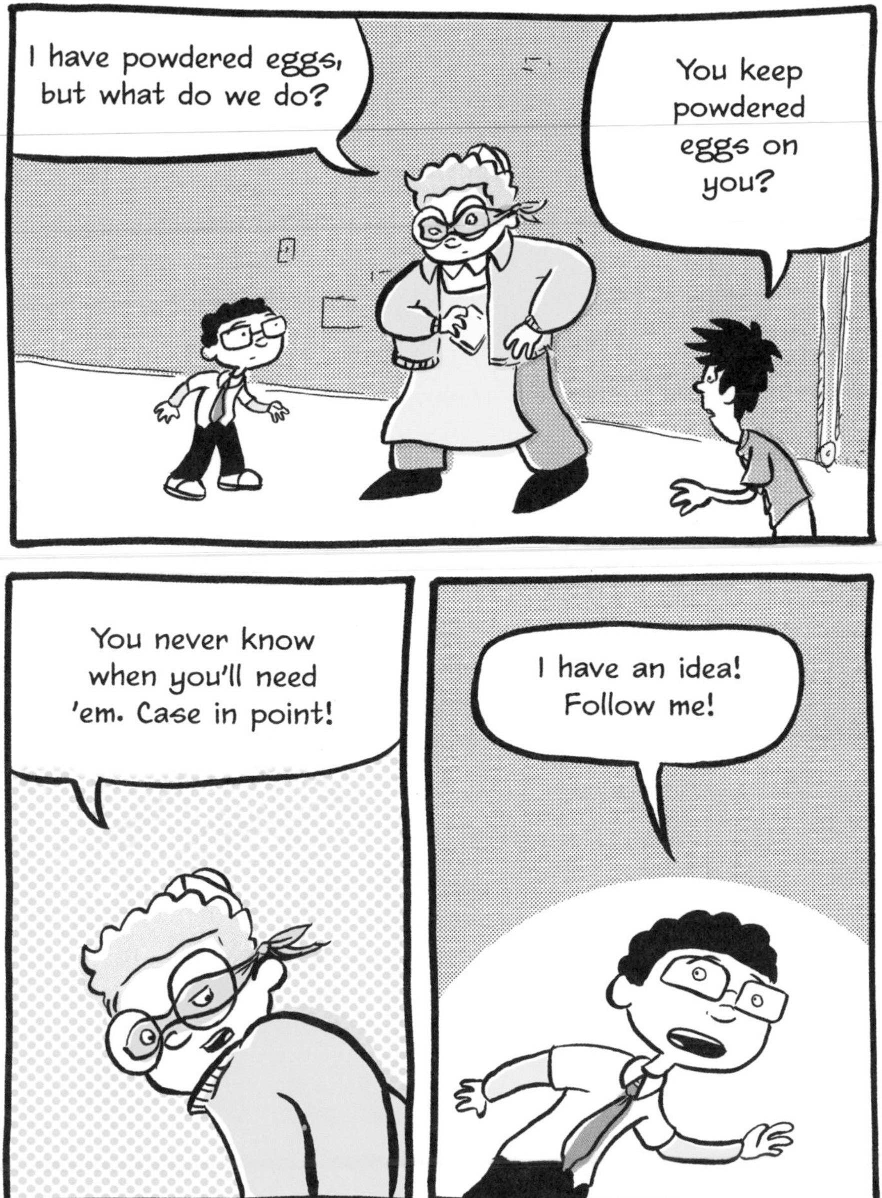
I have powdered eggs, but what do we do?
You keep powdered eggs on you?
You never know when you'll need 'em. Case in point!
I have an idea! Follow me!

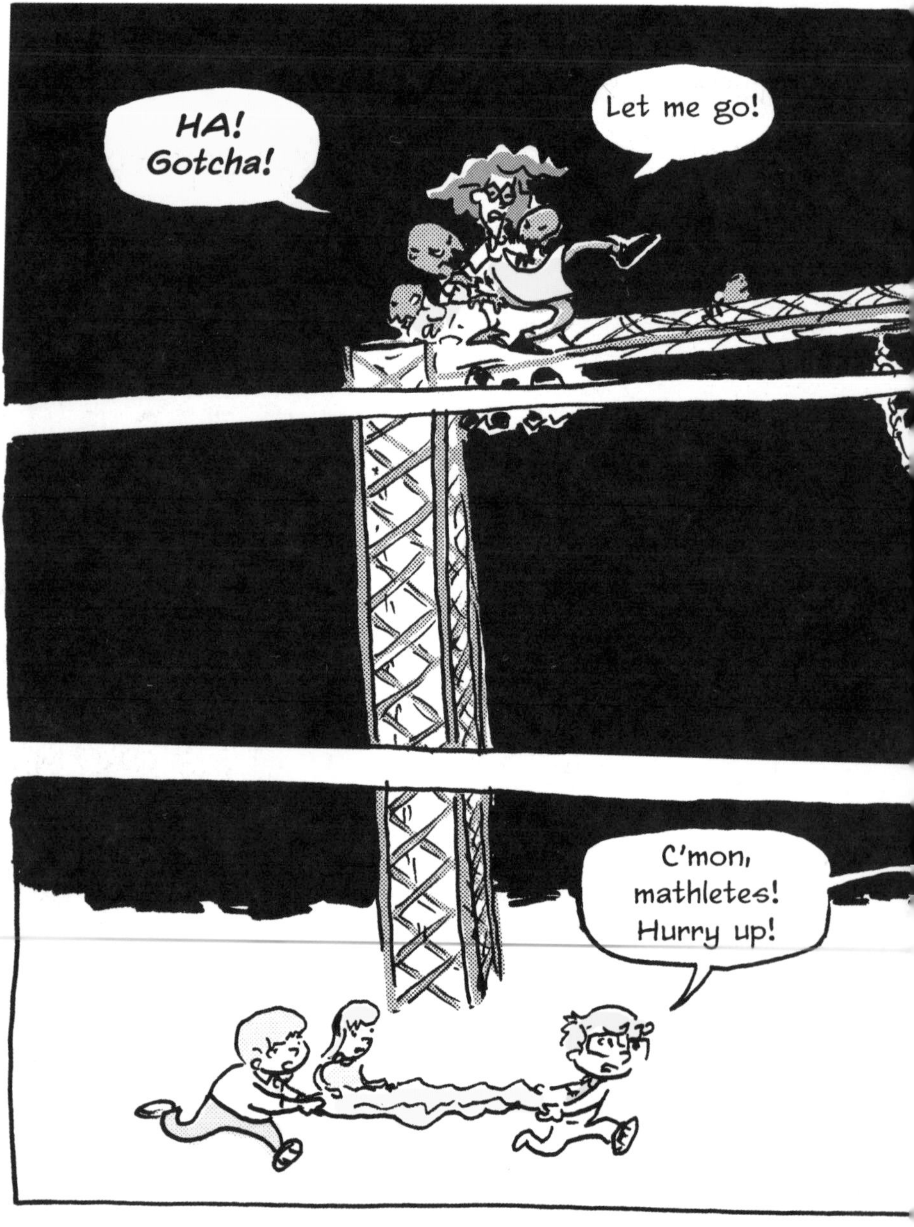
HA! Gotcha!
Let me go!
C'mon, mathletes! Hurry up!

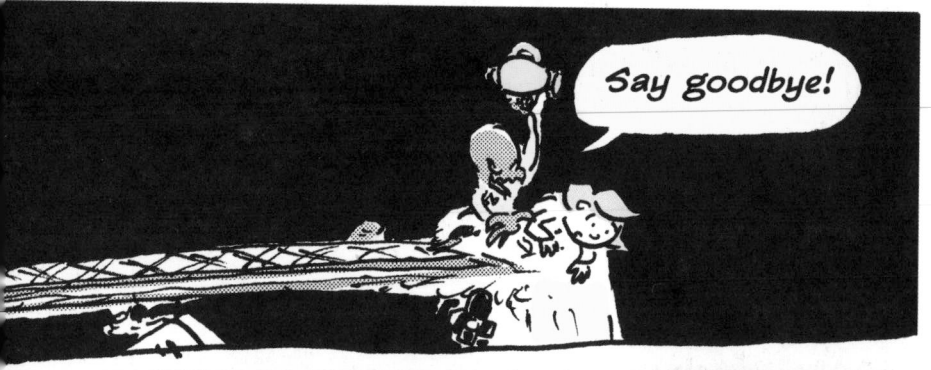

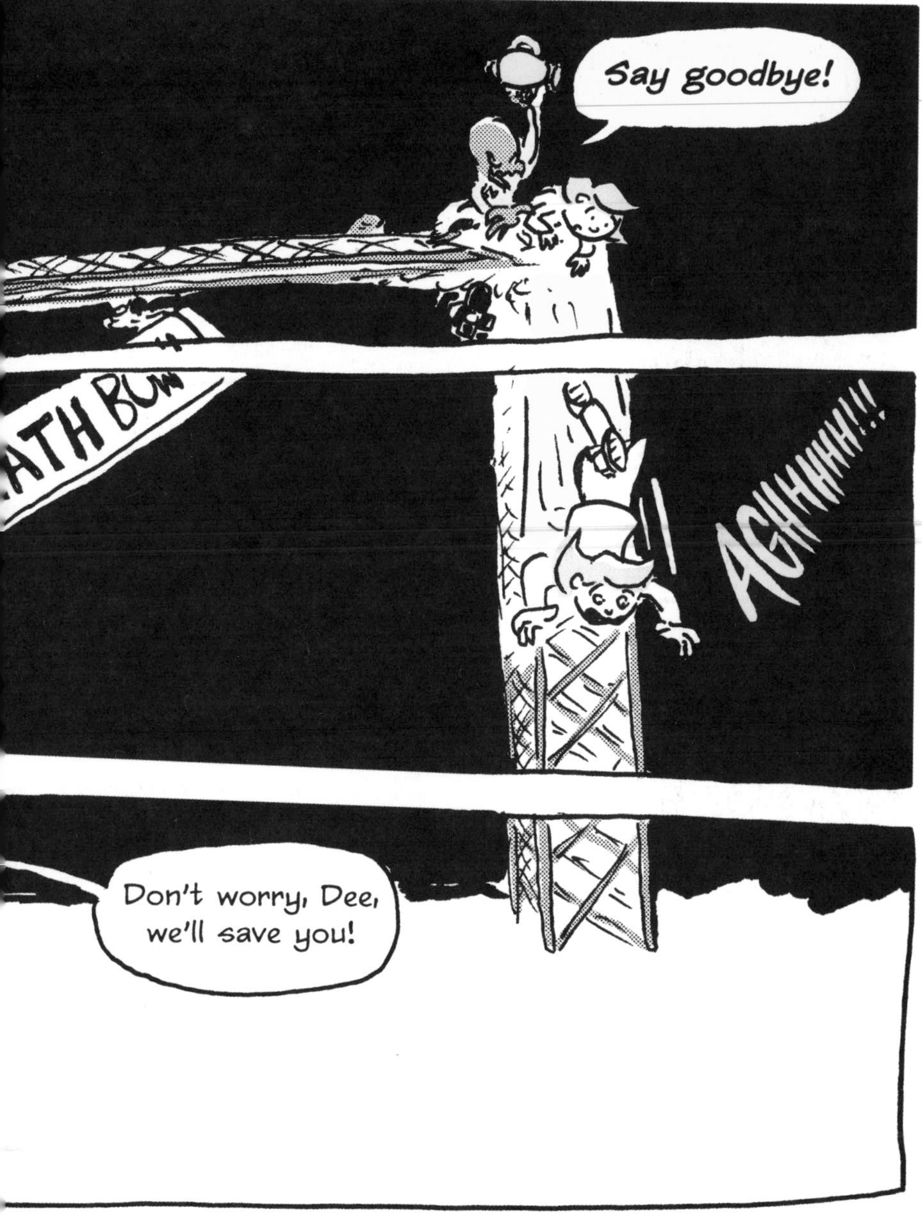

Say goodbye!
AGHHHHH!!!
Don't worry, Dee, we'll save you!

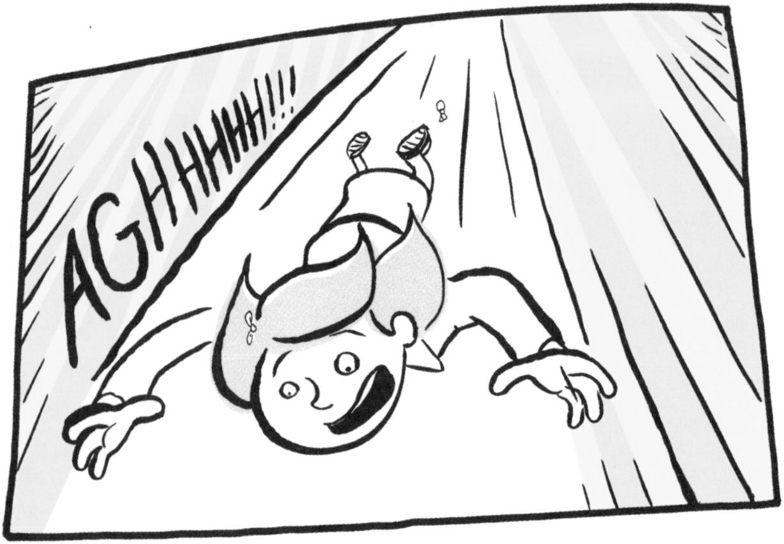
AGHHHHH!!!

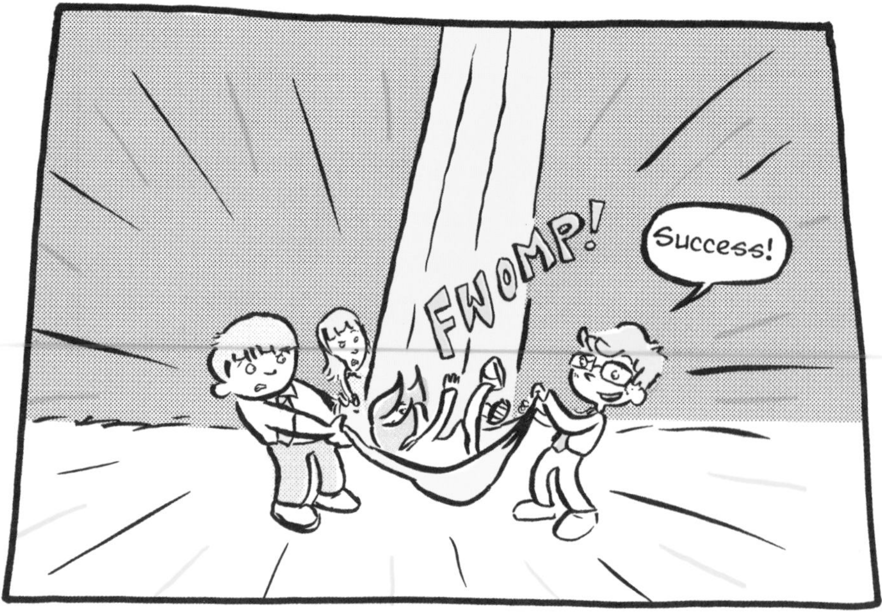
FWOMP!
Success!

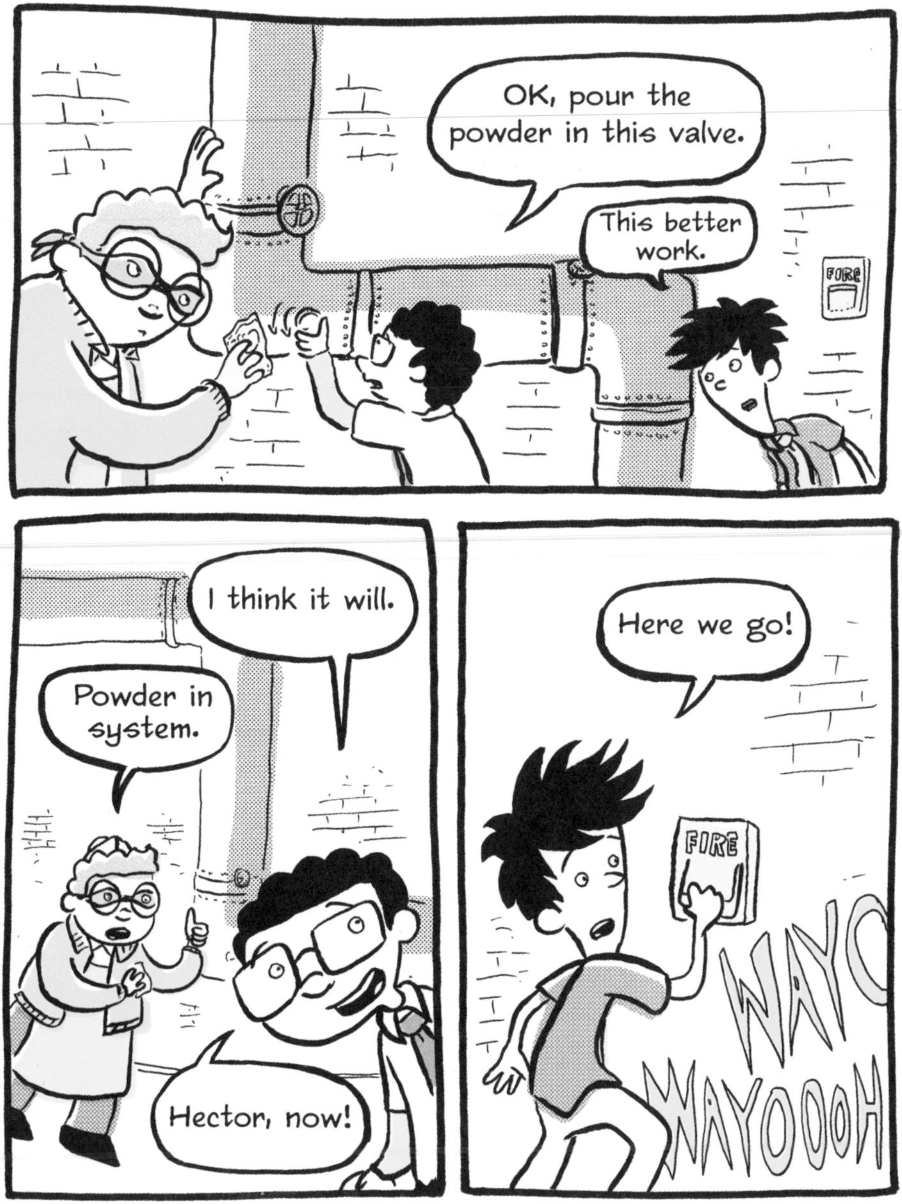
OK, pour the powder in this valve.
This better work.
FIRE
I think it will.
Powder in system.
Hector, now!
Here we go!
FIRE
WAYO
WAYOOOH

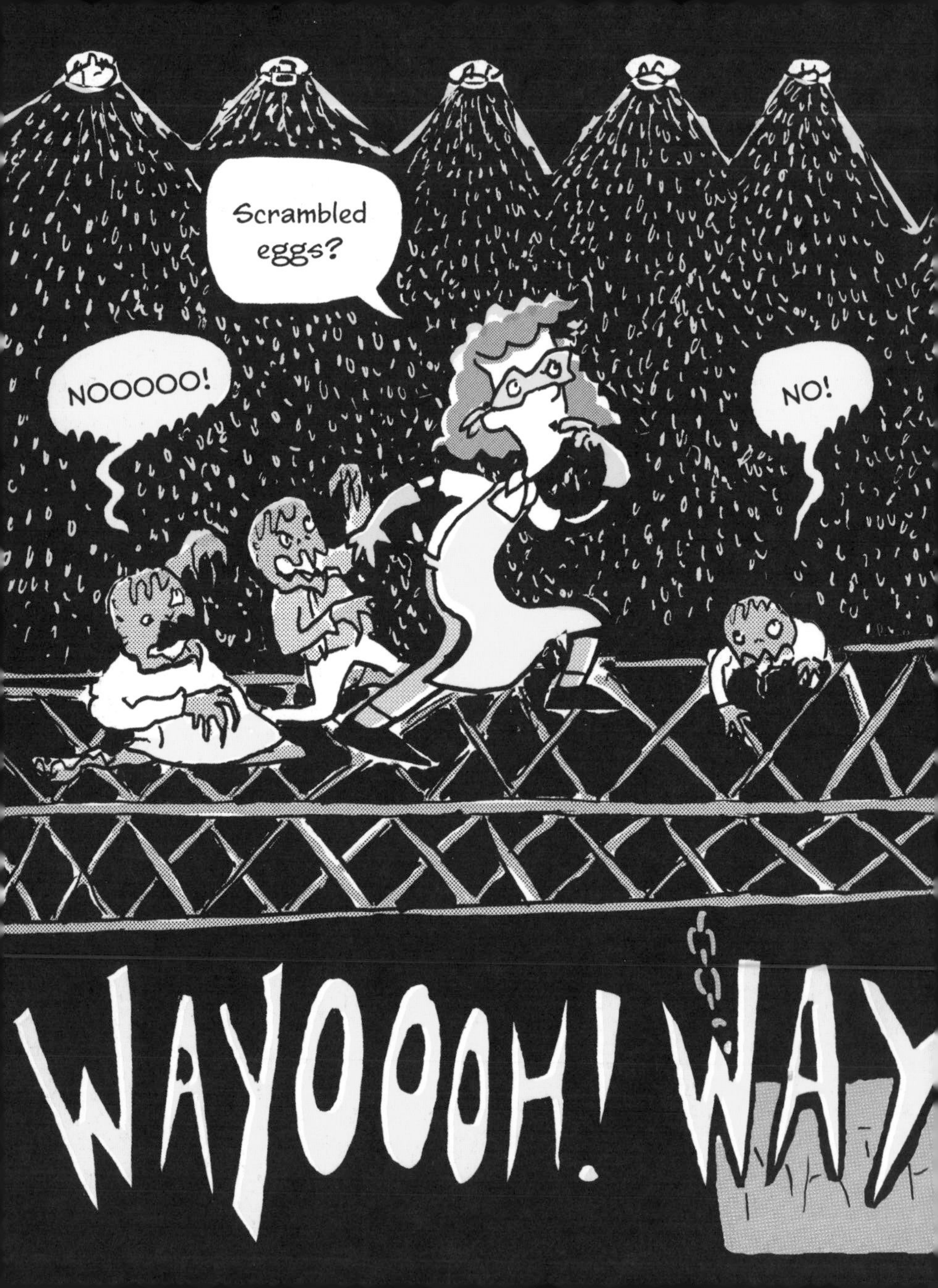
Scrambled eggs?
NOOOOO!
NO!
WAYOOOH! WAY

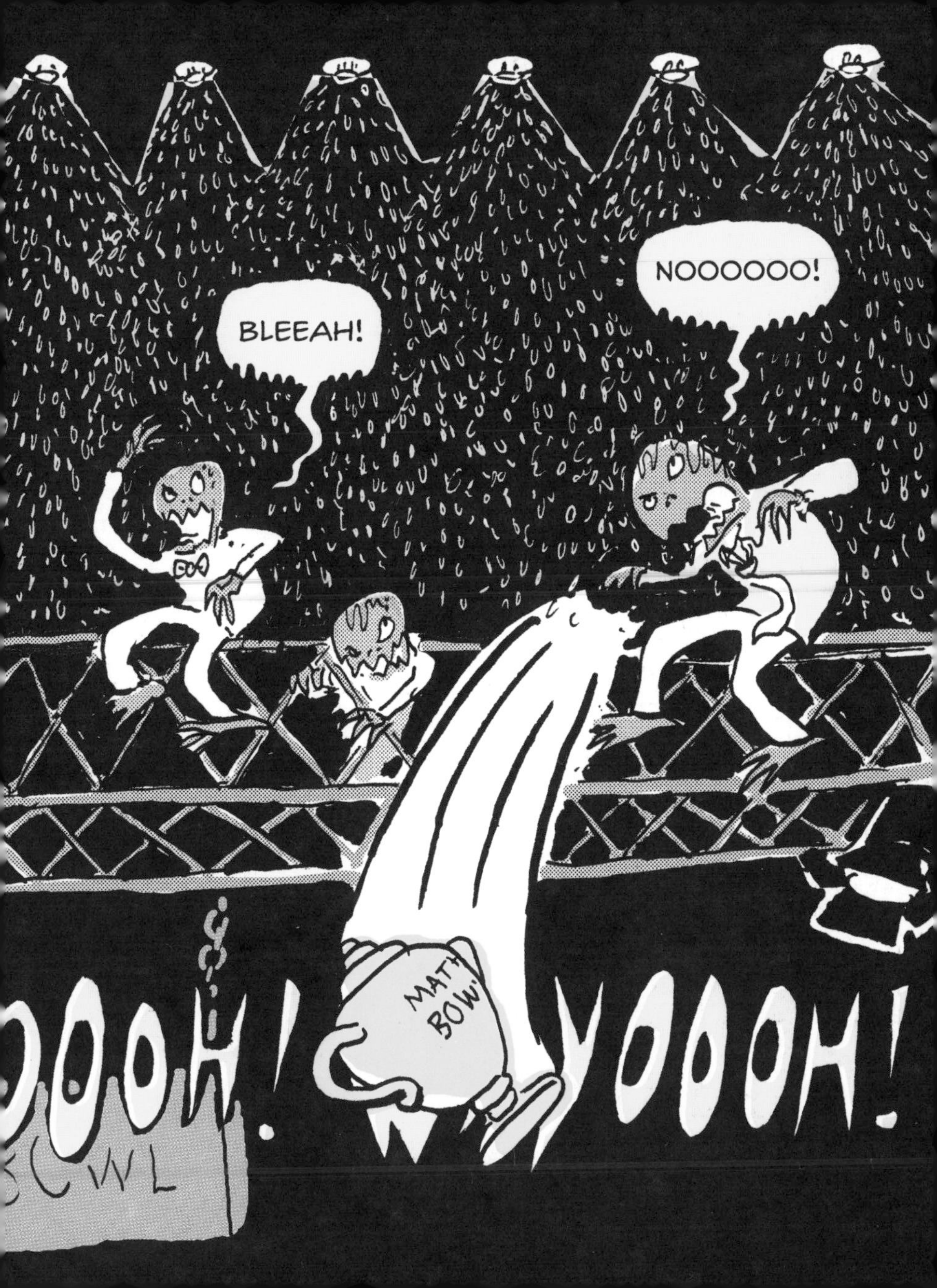
BLEEAH!
NOOOOOO!
OOOH!
MATH BOW
YOOOH!

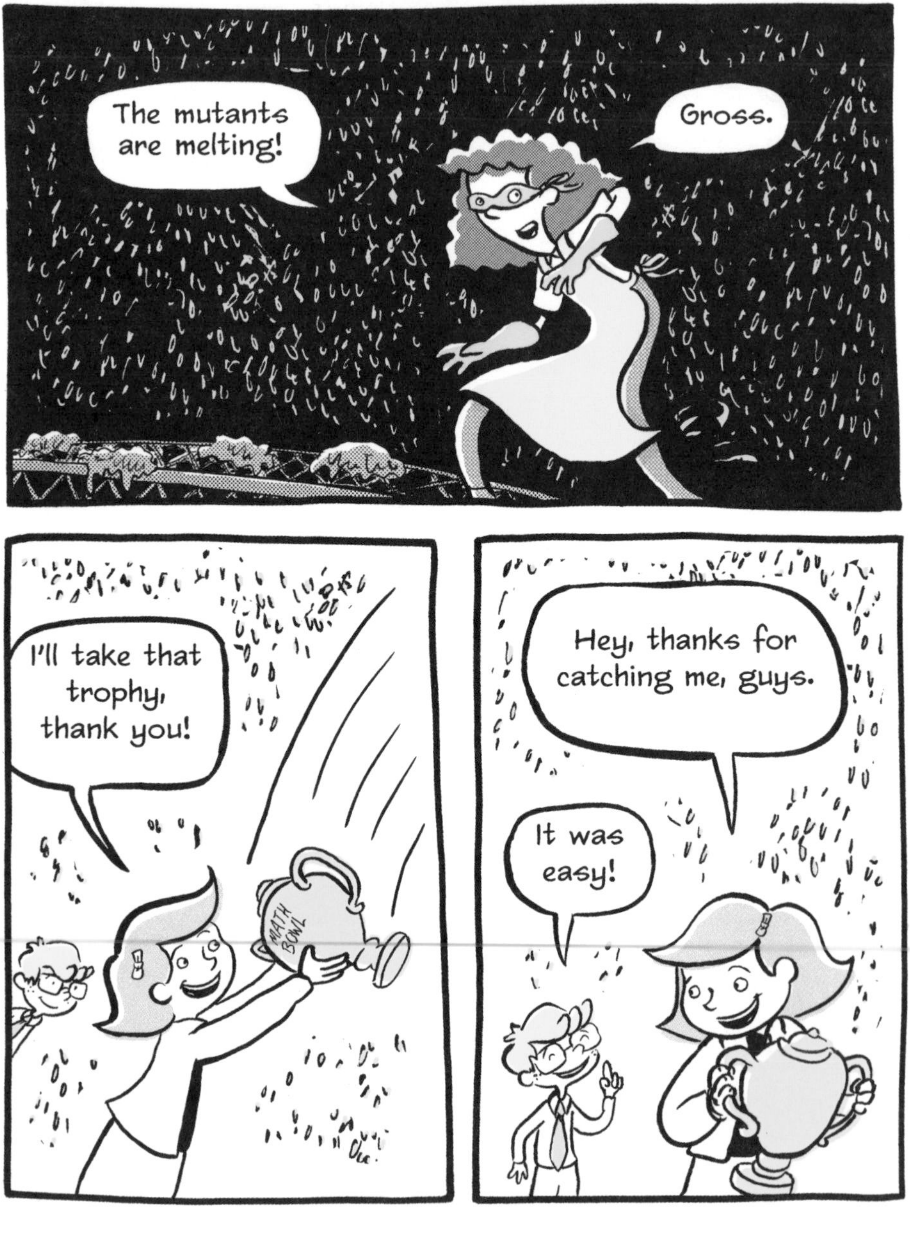
The mutants are melting!
Gross.
I'll take that trophy, thank you!
MATH BOWL
Hey, thanks for catching me, guys.
It was easy!

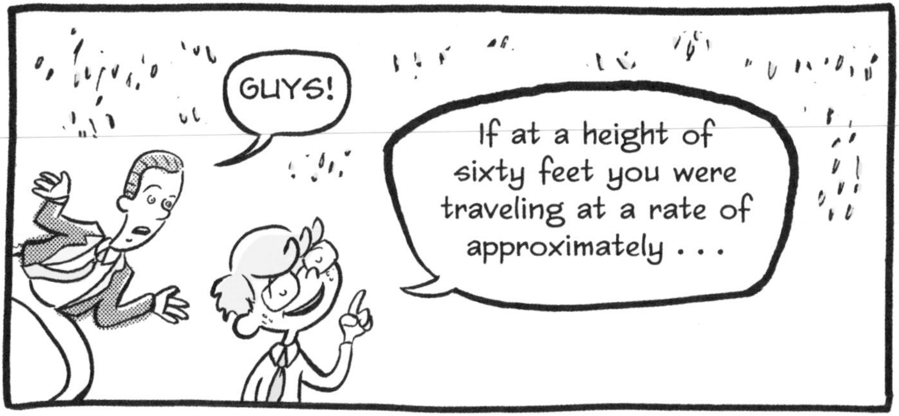
GUYS!
If at a height of sixty feet you were traveling at a rate of approximately . . .

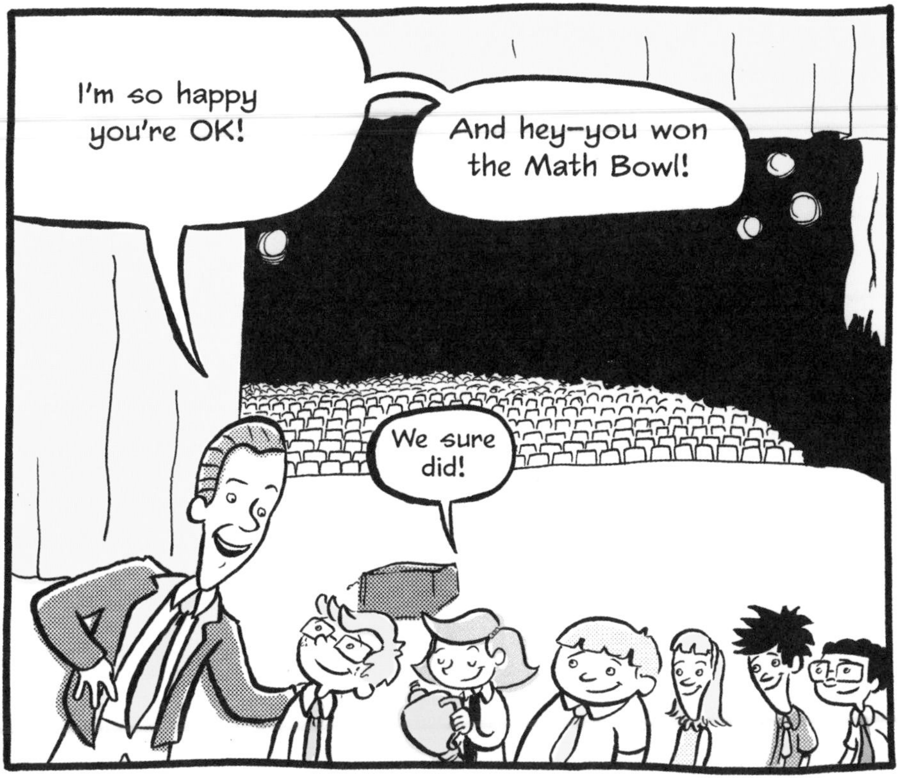
I'm so happy you're OK!
And hey–you won the Math Bowl!
We sure did!

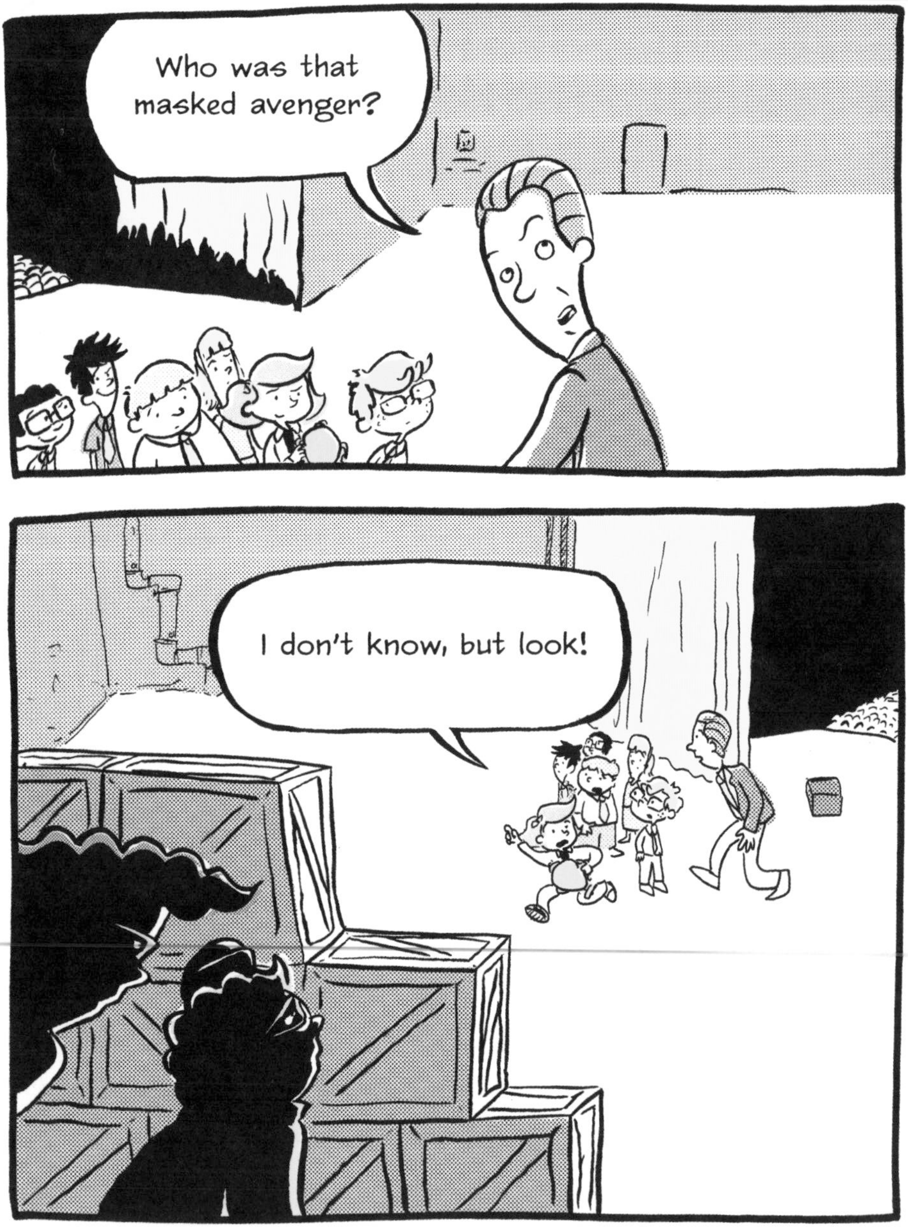
Who was that masked avenger?
I don't know, but look!

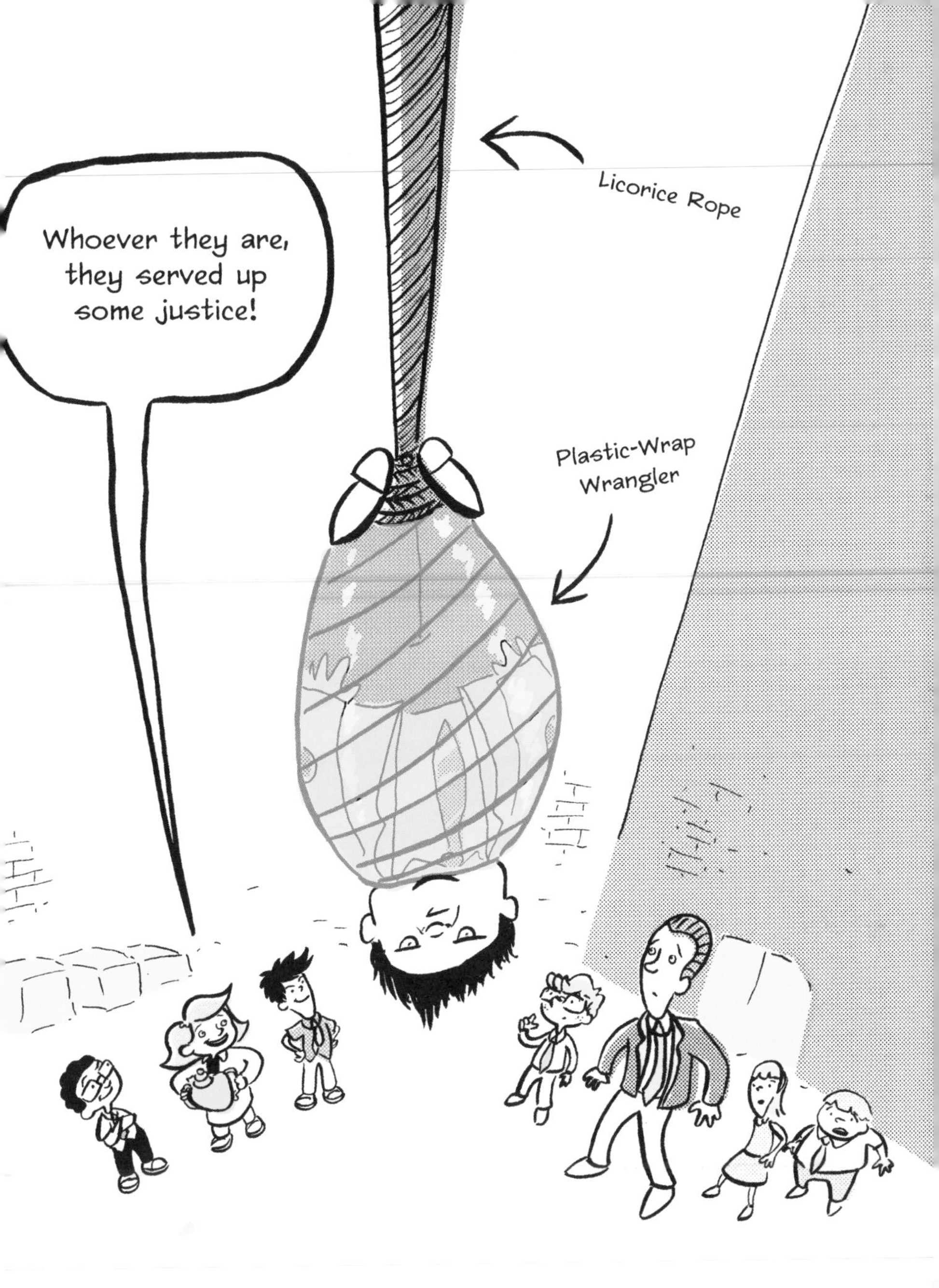
Whoever they are, they served up some justice!
Licorice Rope
Plastic-Wrap Wrangler

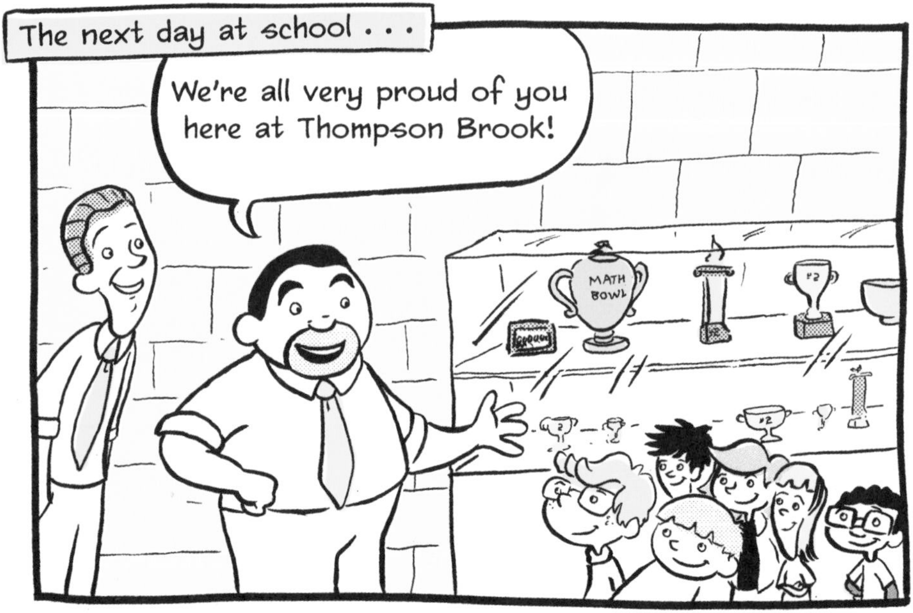
The next day at school . . .
We're all very proud of you here at Thompson Brook!
MATH BOWL

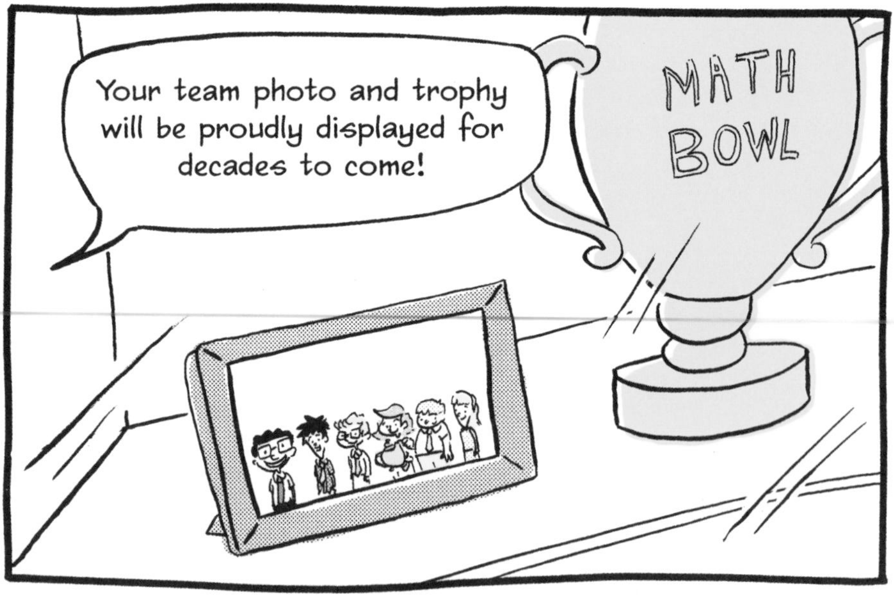
Your team photo and trophy will be proudly displayed for decades to come!
MATH BOWL

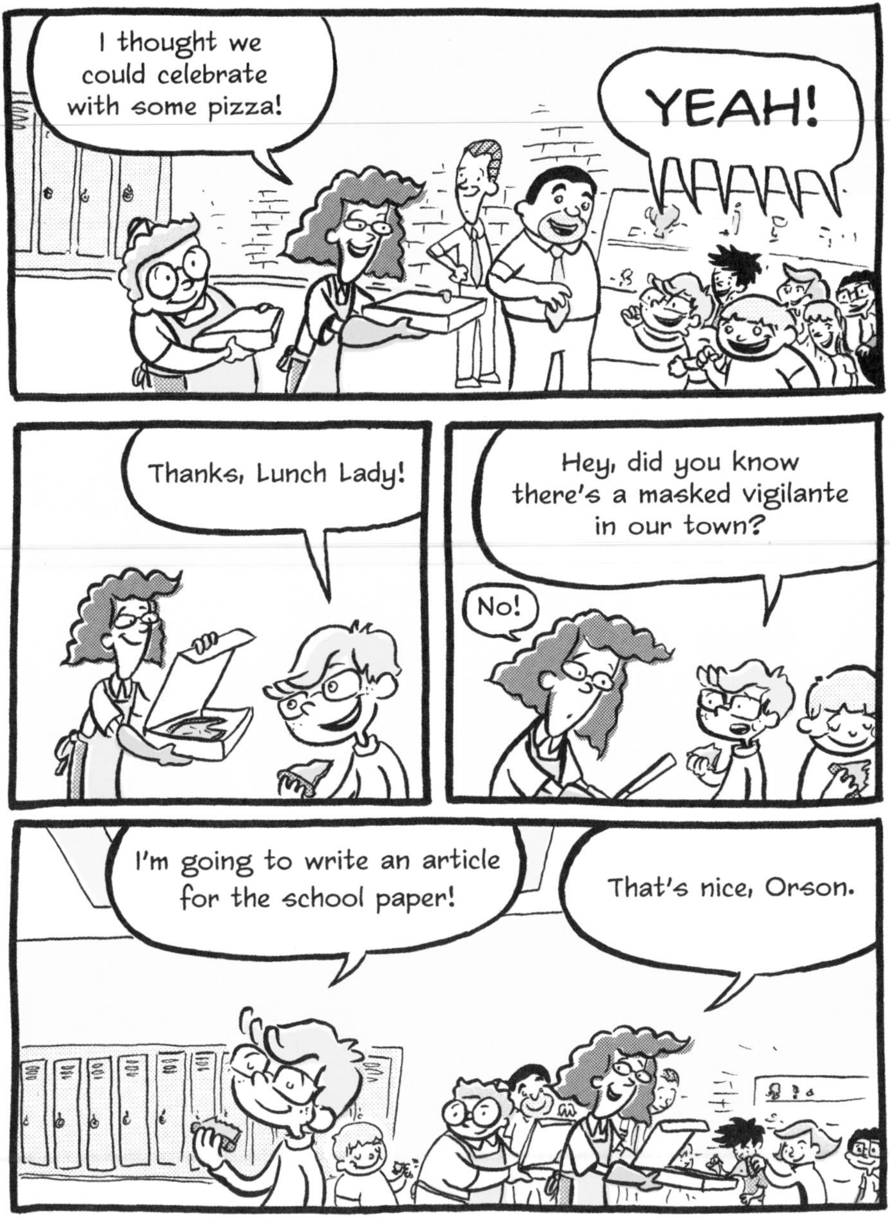
I thought we could celebrate with some pizza!
YEAH!
Thanks, Lunch Lady!
Hey, did you know there's a masked vigilante in our town?
No!
I'm going to write an article for the school paper!
That's nice, Orson.

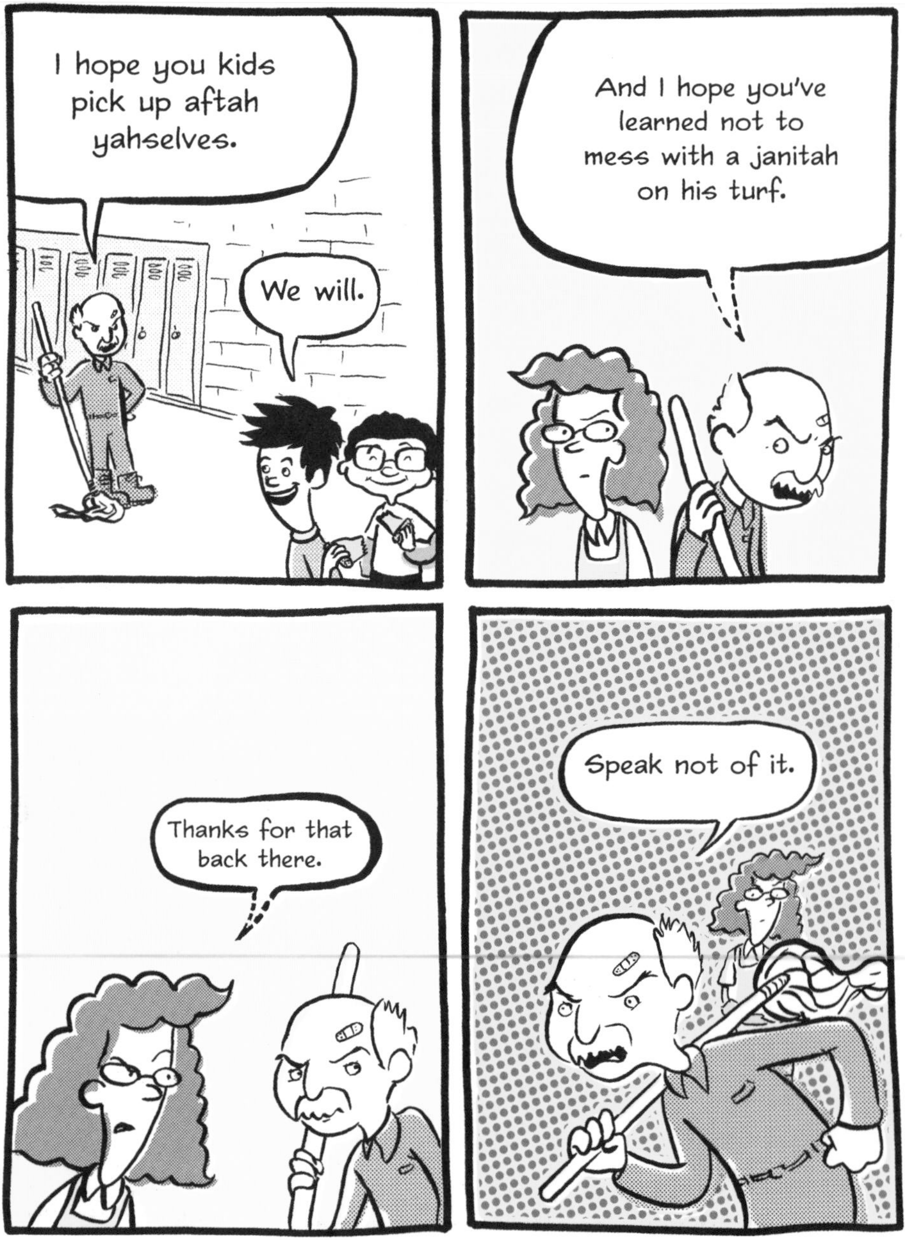
I hope you kids pick up aftah yahselves.
We will.
And I hope you've learned not to mess with a janitah on his turf.
Thanks for that back there.
Speak not of it.

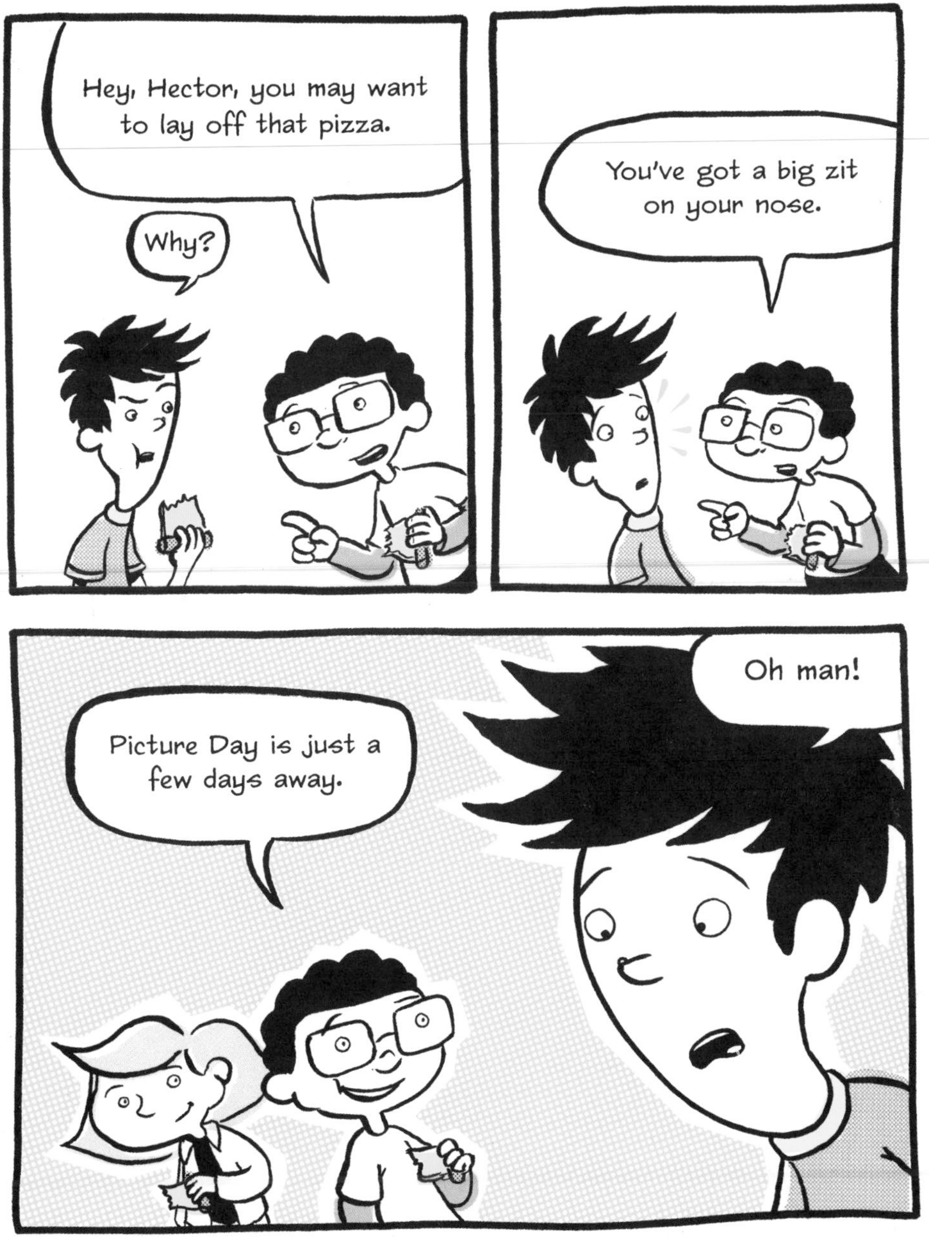
Hey, Hector, you may want to lay off that pizza.
Why?
You've got a big zit on your nose.
Picture Day is just a few days away.
Oh man!

# FOR SIOBHÁN AND PETER

## The author would like to acknowledge the color assist in this book by Joey Weiser and Michele Chidester.

THIS IS A BORZOI BOOK PUBLISHED BY ALFRED A. KNOPF

Visit us on the Web! randomhouse.com/kids

Educators and librarians, for a variety of teaching tools, visit us at randomhouse.com/teachers

*Library of Congress Cataloging-in-Publication Data*
Krosoczka, Jarrett.
Lunch Lady and the mutant mathletes / Jarrett Krosoczka. — 1st ed.
p. cm.
"A Borzoi Book."
Summary: For having skipped the school field trip, Dee, Hector, and Terrence must join the mathletes team, but as they are poised to beat the undefeated champions, secret crime fighter Lunch Lady discovers something strange about the opposing team.
ISBN 978-0-375-87028-6 (trade pbk.) — ISBN 978-0-375-97028-3 (lib. bdg.)
1. Graphic novels. [1. Graphic novels. 2. Competition (Psychology)—Fiction.
3. Mathematics—Fiction. 4. Schools—Fiction. 5. Mystery and detective stories.] I. Title.
PZ7.7.K76Lum 2012
741.5'973—dc23
2011025425

The text of this book is set in Hedge Backwards.
The illustrations were created using ink on paper and digital coloring.

MANUFACTURED IN MALAYSIA
March 2012
10 9 8 7 6 5 4

First Edition